Heike Freiwald

... is mother of two boys. She studied design
at Art Academy in Kassel, Germany. With her children
she later on moved to the USA and got sponsored
by a former senator of Tennessee where
she studied building construction at State Tech. Tennessee.
She opened a fashion boutique and lived in
Tennessee, California, Nebraska and South Dakota
where she restored a centennial farm
in the middle of the prairie in South Dakota.
Years ago she moved back to Germany
and wrote her autobiography ...

"A Nazi's Child is an autobiography
that throws some deep reflections on my life
which was darkened by a Nazi father
and three years of being locked up
in a German reformatory during the 50s.
I became brainwashed, humiliated and
deprived of my identity, freedom, self-esteem, education,
personal belongings and a chance
to communicate with others.
I became a number ..."

(Bildquelle: Archiv/Heike Freiwald)

The love I once so yearned for
is now inside of me.

A Nazi's Child

In Search of my Identity

Autobiography

Heike Freiwald

www.tredition.de

Impressum

© 2012 Heike Freiwald

Umschlaggestaltung, Illustration/*cover design:* Heike Freiwald /
Umschlaggestaltung/technische Produktion/*cover design/technical
production:* DK Agentur/Dietlind Koch-Fecke
Lektorat/Korrektorat, Layout/Produktion/*lectorate/editorial
assistance/ proofreading, layout/production:* DK Agentur/Dietlind
Koch-Fecke

Verlag: tredition GmbH, Mittelweg 177, 20148 Hamburg
Printed in Germany
ISBN: 978-3-8424-8754-3

Bibliografische Information der Deutschen Nationalbibliothek:
Die Deutsche Nationalbibliothek verzeichnet diese Publikation in der
Deutschen Nationalbibliografie; detaillierte bibliografische Daten sind
im Internet über http://dnb.d-nb.de abrufbar.

CONTENTS

© Heike Freiwald, Siegfried Michelt

Preface

A Person's Dignity Should be Inviolable

My story is dedicated to all former institutionalized children from the 50s to the 80s, children who have passed or have been driven to commit suicide, human beings who never became vindicated by German government, church or society.

Due to time our status has changed from being a number to a senior citizen, still burdened by our past of discrimination and injustice. Most of us are still in need of help provided by therapists, in order to find inner peace and freedom.

The fundamental rights did not apply to thousands of German children institutionalized by state and church after Nazi Germany's past war period.

We became isolated from society, stripped of our identity, personal will and freedom, violated on body and soul. We were malnourished, stigmatized and forced to labor without pay.

We became deprived of education, a chance for success in our future.

Most of former institutionalized children never found their purpose in life or a goal to reach and work for. We still are fenced in by former Nazi doctrines that ruled our mind and lives and left us with fear and panic attacks.

We are still treated like second class people and afraid to fall asleep at night in fear of nightmares, reliving the most terrible time of our youth behind bars, without permission to talk or communicate.

Heike Freiwald

Reformatory

It happened on a Friday morning, one week after the incident "At The Hop". Both of my parents were present but avoided to look or even talk to me. All I was told that I did not have to go to work that morning and I wondered why. Shortly after, a car arrived with a woman, introducing herself as a social worker, and that very moment I knew my father had carried out his threat to put me away.

For a moment I was not sure what to think or feel when my suitcase, already packed with my few belongings was brought by my father out of their bedroom where it was hidden. Everything happened kind of in a hurry without the chance for questions. My mother had tears in her eyes and I wondered what would happen to her when I was gone. Who would fetch the doctor at night, and who would buy the grocery at the neighbors store asking to run a tab? It was almost impossible to think my father would undertake my former chores.

The social worker took my suitcase while walking down the stairs, passing our landlady's closed living room door, usually open as invitation to enter. They most have been gone I thought, feeling a sadness for not having the chance for a good bye. The car door was opened by a driver who had waited downstairs, asking me to sit down in the back, followed by the social worker taking the seat next to me.

My small suitcase became stored behind me, given a few moments more to look at the house where I had spent my youth, growing up with ambivalent feelings and fear for punishment, anticipating my annual visits to the farm and my beloved grandparents, looking forward to the middle of June, when a full bowl of ripe strawberries would await me at my landlady's living room and I would reward her kindness with a bunch of daisies always in bloom around my birthday.

Thinking of both my landlady and daughter I called aunt Lieschen who always had spent comfort in times of sadness or pain, my eyes turned to their window in front of the house above the rhododendron bush where movements behind closed curtains gave away their presents.

I thought about many times when I was asked to join their lunch after school or the dimes slipped into my pocket, and I realized that they could not bear to see me being carried away, it was too hard for them to say good bye.

Would this also mean a good bye to Wulf who had kept on writing letters I so desperately awaited daily. Would they be forwarded to me by my parents. My thoughts of Wulf turned into a wakeup call with questions about my current situation and future time to come. All of a sudden I realized that the threat "reformatory" always had an impact being the maximum punishment of a father's right.

Reformatory, the last word needed for his climactically relief within his rage, that triggered the outburst of the same old story about the glorious years during the NS regime, when Germany was still intact, ruled by order and controlled by a government selected of elite people. I had been bombarded with that story over and over again in times of failing his demands or disobeying his rules, the words had been planted in my mind and still haunting me in reoccurring night mares.

The social worker started a conversation by talking about the length of our ride to "Forest Home". She never mentioned the term "Reformatory", it became transformed into an elusive imagination about a secure and protective environment. I started to ask a lot of questions followed by few answers: Including the first opportunity of my own room, being in the company of lots of girls and given the offer to learn many new crafts. She also gave the impression that I could stay in contact with family and friends by writing letters. That was the answer I had been waiting for, to be able to continue my conversation with Wulf, enough comfort already to face unknown challenges in "Forest Home".

About two hours later we arrived at the small village appearing like a picture postcard, situated at the foot of a larger mountain range and created by its community to an idyllic environment with its focus to the old Lutheran church dominating the market place. My ambivalent excitement became calmed by the beauty of the new surroundings, consequently connected by myself with my new home.

We left the small village and turned into a "private road" bordered by pine trees on either side, leading us up the hill towards "Forest Home". The closer we got the harder I could feel my heart beat, triggered by the memory of my father's threat and the contrast transmitted by the forests beauty.

Since I was a little girl I had the need for beauty, reaching out for anything to cover up the ugliness I too often had to face. I found beauty provided by nature, beauty in the presents of my grandfather and kind people, beauty in my connection to my love and best friend, even in my imaginative thoughts creating personal happiness I found beauty, a beauty invisible to the eye but absorbed by heart and mind, a beauty to feel secure, understood, but most of all to be loved.

The car had to slow down admonished by the sign: Private Property, no Trespassing! Placed at the beginning of an endless seeming brick wall to the right, only giving view to the very distance, a gabled roof which belonged to the main building, domicile of the house-mother (Mother Superior) administration and various Lutheran nuns to be addressed as sister.

We had reached the main gate secured by a locked rod iron door separating the brick wall, allowing the first glimpse at the building.

The social worker rung the bell and admonished me to obey the sisters to make it easy on myself. A middle-aged sister dressed in a full length black skirt and same colored blouse decorated with a snow white starched collar around her neck, opened the massive wooden entrance door on top of a few stairs. While approaching us, she carried herself somehow majestically upright without a smile, and I thought probably due to the seemingly uncomfortable bonnet covering the entire head, leaving just enough space for the face to be seen.

This was my first encounter with one of the sisters appearing in her daily black outfit, called habit, completed by the wedding ring on her finger, the symbol to be married to Jesus Christ as a reward for her dedication to defy all earthly temptations.

We were greeted and told that Mother Superior already was expecting us.

The social worker took my small suitcase for the last time in one hand, and my arm with the other as we followed the sister up the few stairs into the hallway. Maybe she meant to show a few sympathy by her touch, except her eyes revealed the same different unspoken knowledge I already had sensed this morning while saying good bye to my mother, a knowledge yet unknown to me.

While entering the huge paneled entry hall, my eyes became focused at the almost full sized statue of "The All Mighty" nailed to the cross, the largest wooden crucifix I had ever seen. It hung in opposite to the entry door, against the back wall and transmitted an instant kind of guilt, similar to the one I had carried with me throughout my youth, never knowing why and what to expect. My feelings even intensified after the entry door became locked and I felt helpless, helpless in front of the judge mental presents of "The All Mighty".

Mother Superior had asked the social worker into her office while I had to wait outside, observing the voluminous interior of the hall, tempted to sit down, but uncertain about consequences. Instead I walked along the walls, gazing at all the pictures depicting paintings of the twelve apostles.

Everything appeared to be too overwhelming since I had arrived, the perfect white starched collar and bonnet of the first sister made absolutely sense, emphasizing order and perfection automatically existing throughout the presents of "The Good Lord".

The social worker left in a hurry and I was asked to enter Mother Superior's room, decorated in the same manner like the entry hall, except this time the crucifix of a much smaller size placed at the wall behind her chair. She welcomed me at Forest Home and told me that from now on I would be number 830.

Within seconds my identity became exchanged by digits, burned into my mind, an object marked by an authority willing to manifest their doctrines behind locked doors, yet under the protective cover of false pretension. What is left of a girl without a name, a Jane Doe, with the exception of being alive, punished by separation from society, locked behind closed doors.

I was told by Mother Superior to wait in the entry hall to be picked up by a sister who would take me to the place for new-comers.

In order to get there, we left through the back door and crossed the premises where I could count several more buildings in visible distance to each other, connected by well-groomed walk ways shadowed by huge trees.

On our way I was told to read the regulation sheet thoroughly, handed to me by Mother Superior, several pages depicting the house rules of Forest Home. I did not listen to the same advise already admonished by the social worker, my attention was focused on the large ring where several keys lined up by length gave away a certain rattle to each of her steps, a similar noise I had noticed before when meeting the first sister.

During my entire time within Forest Home, being rotated around several "Stations" (buildings) my fear only was connected with the key chains, the miracle weapon against my personal freedom, resistant to expressions of personal feelings. Many times I would dare to verbal disagreement about unfair punishment to other girls or to myself, the proof of my unbroken spirit while accepting the punishment of utter silence behind a locked door, not knowing when I would be released again to the group.

One of the keys had opened the door to the building where new arrivals, so called "gefallene Mädchen" (bad girls) had to start a new life away from civilization, yet becoming civilized by obeying rules they were told. Rules of former discipline and order I already had lived by as demand of my father.

The sister took my small suitcase away from me and opened the door to the "workroom" where I faced girls different of age placed along the wall, sitting on a chair, forming a circle. Each of them was wearing a similar looking grey outfit, an oversized dress almost touching their same colored slippers made of felt. About thirty girls just looked at me without saying a word while being occupied with different hand craft. Only their eyes revealed individual emotions and questions I only could imagine.

Inside the circle, placed in the center of the room, an oval shaped table was occupied by two sisters on either end, resembling the appearance of the others I already had met. I felt like being mustered by them from top to toe above the rim of their glasses, and I knew that my reaction by showing a smile would be the wrong timing while being introduced to the group as: 830.

One of the two sisters pointed to the empty chair next to her while asking if I was familiar with needle work, being able to embroider my number 830 onto labels sewn into the cloth I would have to wear, my grey institutional clothing.

At school I always had performed well during needle work class and therefore capable of fulfilling the task. It was an awkward situation sensing the curious looks of some girls while sitting next to a sister with watchful and observing eyes towards the group, plus observing the result of my work. She seemed to be satisfied, nodded her head and said: "Gut so." – (ok).

On my first afternoon in Forest Home I embroidered 830 numerous times with red threat onto a small white ribbon to be cut into labels.

Sometimes in between my work, I would look around without turning my head, trying to read bottled up emotions behind seemingly sad and voiceless faces. Nobody talked, yet conversed with their eyes, and sometimes one could hear a timid giggle to be silenced at once by the sharp reaction of a sister threatening punishment. Soon I learned about different kind of punishment connected with different kind of rules.

To be caught talking to each other during the day while working could mean to be excluded from meals or the group, locked up in your room alone with nothing to do but reading the Bible.

When I entered my room that very first evening I just was stunned by its interior: an iron bed, a chair, a metal washbowl filled with water on top a wooden console. A small towel with dark blue stripes, apparently cut from the same fabric that covered blanket and pillow upon my bed, was neatly hung over the metal bar connected to the right side of the console. The floor was made of wood, waxed and polished to a shine I never ever had achieved while working the stairway at home. A chamber pot, half visible to the eye while hidden below the bed, eliciting my very first smile that very day, a small relief to my jitters triggered by the vertical iron bars covering the outside of my small window.

I sat down on the chair, almost afraid of using the bed with its creaseless cover and thought about the girls who might have occupied this room before me, consequently sensing their pain and tears resulting from helplessness. Yes, I felt helpless, and like many moments before I thought of my grandfather's love, the only remedy that could ease my feelings. The same time I thought of Wulf and looked for the small suitcase, carrying my most important possession, my writing paper with matching envelopes, a few stamps and my fountain pen.

What had happened to my personal belongings? My first impulse was to ask the sister. I turned around and noticed the closed door behind me without detecting a door handle. In my amazement about the tiny room I had missed the sound of the turning key, locking my door from the outside.

For the first time I finally understood my father's threat. I was locked up in a tiny room, a cell where a locked door with missing inside door handle and a barred window would become a daily reminder of being a fallen girl.

What had I done to deserve such severe punishment? Why was I incarcerated like a prisoner, stripped of my identity, silenced like a free bird kept in a cage? In times like this I always could reach for the only remedy that would return my strength and willpower: Friederich, my grandpa, whose love and former teachings about the beauty of nature would let me forget my pain for a while.

That very first evening in Forest Home I promised myself to endure, even beat this kind of inhuman punishment with a spirit strengthened by the memory of a man with a wide-open heart for Love.

I still had remained on the chair thinking about my life, when dusk became changed by dark and the bare light bulb at the ceiling was turned on from the outside, spending just enough light to read the document listing the so called "house rules."

Again, I was overwhelmed by total disbelieve about the dos and don'ts leaving no space for any personal freedom. Each day had a strict, regimental timing starting with the ring of the bell at 6am as a wakeup call.

A sister would walk along the long hall way unlocking the doors next to each other before she had switched off the bell. Besides waking up the girls, the bell was connected with each room, hindering anyone to leave without becoming detected. There was no snoozing left in the morning, one had to hurry to line up outside in front of the door carrying the chamber pot while still wearing the institutional night gown.

The line would move slowly toward the end of the hall way where each chamber pot became controlled by a sister before one had to empty its contents into the only toilette located at our floor. After that, one had to hold the pot below the faucet to receive some water for rinsing, controlled again by the sister who made sure that nobody had used their pot for a bowel movement, otherwise one had to accept punishment. All chamber pots became piled up to be cleaned later by the girl assigned for duty and placed in front of each door with one's personal number pointed to the front.

Three times a day one could use the toilette, before breakfast, lunch and dinner, given each time three small pieces cut from an old newspaper.

All of the sudden the light went out, it must have been 8pm and I only had read part of the paper. This would be the last time wearing my own clothing; tomorrow I would look no different from all the others, dressed in a grey institutional uniform representing the reformatory, my future prison, blinding the ignorant public with its comforting name: Forest Home.

The window inside my room obviously had a different function to a regular one. Besides the bars, its location was high up at the wall, only to be reached by using the chair in order to take a closer look at the outside. When I had entered my room that evening, the small opening only gave view to some branches of a tree growing in front and I was ready to look at the entire picture. By using the chair as a ladder I was able to admire the huge tree with arms reaching out to the bars in front of my window like holding on to it. That very moment I had found the only friend who would interrupt some silent nights by stretching its branches through the bars, saying hello with its soft brush against the window, soothing my loneliness.

For a moment I felt content and disconnected from my worries while thinking of my grandfather who had introduced me to beauty I always had searched for and found during times of personal agony and despair. Before I laid down, my last view lingered for a while at the small wooden cross hung at the wall above my bed, its simplicity revealed by the moonlight.

It was still early, the time of day when people at the outside would enjoy the rest of their free time with varies entertainment, and my thoughts went back to a few days I had enjoyed myself together with other teenagers "At the Hop" dancing, talking enthusiastically about our musical heroes while gazing at the boys who never could compare to the one I loved. I started to wonder how Wulf could possibly react if he found out about myself being deprived of my freedom and distant from society for my own good, so to speak.

The public always had a certain image about a Reformatory as the place where bad kids would be sent to be reformed, children who had failed to obey the law or their parents, children who had ended up in the gutter. Knowing about the ignorant and prejudiced public opinion, Forest Home would haunt me for the rest of my life, no matter how the judgment about my person was based on controversial facts, unfair in my mind. Tomorrow I would write a detailed letter to Wulf about my father's decisive action, it would make him understand without being judge mental.

The length of my staying at Forest Home was uncertain to me, based on the improvement of my character I was told, a reason to question myself if Wulf would wait for me until I become released, a question that would torture my mind that very night and in many more to come. Before I finally fell asleep I realized that my thoughts were free, untamable, undetectable, the only personal possession left to me.

The next morning the sound of the terrible bell with its jarring sound announced a new day to learn about the rules of Forest Home.

Still half asleep I stumbled out of bed and lined up outside holding my chamber pot in front of me after the door became unlocked, thinking about the dos and don'ts so far read. To watch everybody dressed in their oversized institutional nightgowns, holding their night bowls away from their bodies like one would hold a dead mouse, was actually a reason to laugh if it had not been such sad reality.

A chamber pot was nothing new to me since I was a little girl, able to walk, sharing my parents' bedroom. Every night my father picked it up from underneath his side of the bed and placed it on the same spot it had been put the night before, in front of the small crease separating their two beds. Sometimes I would talk, half asleep while using the chamber pot, enabling my father to ask all sorts of questions, consequently revealing negative or positive things I had done or not done. And sometimes I would get punished for things I knew better not to do but unable to resist, wondering how my father could have found out.

Again, it was a sad picture to watch some girls still half asleep, carrying their pots with one hand while using the other to free their face from a few strands of untamed hair. It took a while to overcome the shame I endured each morning while walking the line to the end of the hall way, where a sister would make or ruin my day, depending on the contents of my chamber pot.

After my pot was controlled and piled up with the others, I was handed a bucket filled with water, a floor and dusting cloth for cleaning my room, an everyday routine I would get used to. The document had especially pointed out to be thorough about the job, a sister would do daily rounds, checking the cleanliness of one's room while using a glove.

This chore was nothing new to me either, having cleaned our kitchen, bedroom and stairwell at home controlled by the watchful eyes of my father, already had taught me to give it my all in order to avoid punishment. I did not mind crawling underneath the bed in order to reach each corner, and I did not mind to clean myself afterwards with a small washcloth while standing naked in front of the small washbowl filled with cold water, come summer or winter.

My worries were connected with the moment a rattling key chain would announce the sister on her way to my room, and the noise of all different key chains would develop a phobia still appearing in night-mares. It was the second day and I remembered having exactly one hour for cleaning the room and myself, plus getting dressed before the sister would open the door to let us out.

This time we had to line up two girls next to each other, dressed in our institutional clothing, guarded by two sisters, one in the front and the other at the end. Somehow it was a similar scenario to soldiers marching on their way to their exercise, guarded by two sergeants. Our group resembled the same regimental behavior without an enthusiastic song coming from our lips and wooden shoes on our feet. We were accompanied by utter silence, a silence that unleashes physical pain after days and days of endurance.

We had crossed the premises and walked towards a small wooden building considered "The Chapel" to participate at the daily worship, held each morning by Mother Superior at 7am. Several groups from different stations already gathered in front the door still locked, showing a nosy interest towards us newcomers while waiting for the House Mother to unlock the building.

It seemed like each moment of the day was connected with a certain rule, and this time it was ours to become incorporated into the group, to be the last to enter, to be seated in the first row. The Chapel was furnished with long wooden benches placed in the middle with just enough space to sit without the comfort of a backrest.

This time the sisters used the chairs lined up against the wall on either side of the benches in order to overlook the rows and check on us girls.

Altogether Forest Home had so called 150 inmates, girls of various ages and of various backgrounds.

Some of us were orphans, pushed around from one family to another, consequently ending up with the wrong people. Some had committed a petty crime without being given a second chance. Some older girls had become influenced by the wrong person, helplessly ending up in the gutter. And a few of us just unlucky by having picked the wrong parents, altogether a reason to be locked up behind bars, to become reformed?

Reformed by sisters who were chosen or had decided to be chosen to rescue lost young souls with the two words: discipline and order, without realizing that those two words were once idealized by people wearing the same colored clothing, reforming by exchanging identities with numbers, killing behind fences without knowledge to the public.

We did not have to face the ultimate punishment, we only got robbed of our chances to develop a brilliant mind or explore the hidden gifts inside of us. Only a few of us had a future chance in life, only the strong ones who did not accept the daily brainwash while afraid of punishment, punishment covered up by The Holy Book, The Bible.

In the beginning of my stay in Forest Home my feelings about the Sisters became based on my imaginative connection to their dedication, I respected them because of the idealistic conviction to help wherever needed, an important principle based on their holy order. After a time of effortless tries to elicit at least a smile from their faces which automatically would influence and change their inflexibility, my opinion towards sisters with the image of virgin living did not balance their attitude towards young people who needed help instead of receiving punishment.

To live with my new acknowledgement helped to ease my frustration, made it much easier to endure their daily brainwash and punishment. I had freed myself from the barrier to their emotions, their aura had vanished, leaving an opponent who tried to oppress myself.

My respect had changed to dislike, I actually needed to hate, to defend myself with the second strongest weapon next to love. I tried so hard to unleash my feelings, to find the trigger leading to the eruption I needed inside of me. In times of struggle my mind automatically had always reached for my grandfather. In this case my memories of his unconditional love plus teachings about goodness in people and his love to the All Mighty had now become the blockage to such need; grandfather had interfered, I was unable to hate.

All I could do is to show my dislike to oppose their teachings and false pretensions, knowing about the consequences, but willing to take. Each day we were forced to read and learn several chapters depicted by the Bible, the only access I ever had to written words besides the Hymnbook during my entire stay of three years.

Our group was the last to enter the Chapel, where Mother Superior already had stepped onto the platform, silently overlooking the room above her gold rimmed glasses. By towering the entire crowd due to the three steps, her voluminous figure personified the incarnation of strictness, discipline and toughness in contrast to her bonnet that never seemed to keep its place, adding a funny touch to her entire radiance. Maybe that was the reason I would always respect her for adding some amusement subconsciously to my ambivalent feelings combined of fear and the need for acceptance.

She acknowledged the group by saying: "Good morning, let us worship."

After having prayed the "Vater Unser" (Lord's Prayer) we were permitted to sit down before picking up a Hymnbook already placed on the bench. We always had to share one book with the girl sitting to our right, trying hard to find any opportunity for a verbal contact, to be punished if noticed.

That very morning during one hour of "Worship" I learned an important rule that might help to achieve some positive acknowledgement from Mother Superior and all the other sisters. I would have to study various chapters from the Bible thoroughly every day in order to avoid embarrassment as well as punishment in front of the entire group.

Each morning after Worship, Mother Superior would select a specific chapter or prayer for us to learn by heart in the solitary of our room, disconnected from the real world, alone with our own worries, afraid of being asked to recite the studies the next morning.

What a difference to the wonderful memories about Sunday mornings when grandpa would take me by my hand and let me carry his Bible on our way to church where both of us would worship in our own way. Grandpa in his modest way by using his sonorous voice to reveal his love and entire conviction to the "All Mighty", while I was busy to admire grandpa's powerful body, trying to please him by singing more powerful than necessary.

Each evening during my studies and pressure learning about the Written Word, I remembered the time when I looked forward to Sunday mornings, excited and free spirited, not afraid of anything in the presence of my grandfather who opened up my mind and interest about The Good Lord by living it.

To be locked up, stripped of one's identity and free spirit is a challenge on one's conviction, belief and trust. Here I was forced to broaden my horizon about the Bible connected with various consequences. I either could please by pretending or convince with enthusiasm, or fail by acting resentfully, consequently receiving punishment, usually by being exempt from meals during an entire day.

Well, I tried to go along with the rules, avoiding unnecessary trouble since it was easy for me to learn and the only chance to read. Besides, I always was hungry and waited for the sisters on duty to look for their watches when I thought it was time for either lunch or dinner. There was no clock to check the time of day except one could manage to glimpse at the sister's wristwatch and pass it on to the group by using sign language.

We were deprived of the most simple needs, left in ignorance about everything, especially the day of our individual release.

I had to live with all the lies and false information given by the social worker on my way to Forest Home. There was no schooling or writing to my boyfriend, no chance of making new friends, no personal possessions or books, only memories were left for myself, unreachable for anyone to steel or forbid.

During my first participation at the morning Worship I could sense the tension released by some girls who did not care to do their homework in hope not to become called By Mother Superior to recite the part of the Bible requested by her. The entire room was filled with voiceless young girls, expressing their emotions through body talk and wondering eyes. The atmosphere was concentrated with hidden fear and rejection, opposite to the calm and peaceful moments in church next to grandpa, whose unspoken love always made me take his hand.

The Worship ended with Mother Superior's daily prayer, usually involving her concern and hope for us, her protégées, to search our souls and transform our sinful lives with prayers for forgiveness, plus by reading the Bible. After Mother Superior had worked herself carefully down the three steps of her narrow platform, she straightened out her bonnet and walked back in an upright walk towards the main building, her oversized Bible carried close to her huge bosom.

The rest of us left the building the same we had entered, row by row in perfect manner without saying a word. Outside, each group gathered and walked in perfect formations back to their individual housing, one sister leading the way, the other one closing the group.

Like I had mentioned before, each part of the day was perfectly timed, and five round tables already were set for breakfast. Our meal in the morning consisting of black (chicory) coffee and two slices of bread, one already spread with margarine, the other one plain to be spread with sugar beet syrup from a bowl placed in the middle of the table. It was the same breakfast served each day during my stay at Forest Home, and each single day I couldn't help but thinking about the home made liver and blood sausage grandma had put on the table next to grandpa's smoked ham and the large decanter of fresh milk.

With my eyes closed, I still could taste all the delicacies my grandparents had dished up in order to put some meat on my bones, grandpa used to say, but most of all to watch me eat with a smile on my face. My dreams became ended after thirty minutes had passed, breakfast time was over and the working day had begun. It was the same as usual for all the girls in my group, to me it became a sad and different one without pre-warning, a day of personal insult I never was able to forget during my entire life.

One of the sisters told me to follow her to see the doctor. I had no idea and questioned why since I was in perfect health, without any symptoms or pain. With my question left unanswered I followed the sister along the hall way to a door with a rectangle polished sign depicting: Doctor Office. The door opened after the sister's knock and I was asked to enter by a different sister dressed as a nurse, telling me to undress and follow the demand of the doctor who stood next to the strange looking chair placed in the middle of the room.

The doctor's age was revealed by his grey hair and stoop posture, obviously an old man having turned insensitive and unkind due to his job examining all newcomers of Forest Home. He examined my chest, my ears plus the condition of my teeth, mumbling the results to the sister who made notes on a piece of paper later added to my personal file. During his examinations I had a chance to look at all the strange looking medical equipment neatly placed on a white towel on top the table next to the chair, starting to wonder about its purpose.

Soon I should find out when asked to lay down on the chair which had become changed into a bed by a mechanism turning the back rest down while moving the foot rest up. I was told to spread my legs and place each into the small opening on top an iron pole connected to both sides in short distance to my pelvis. All of a sudden I got really scared when he took one of the long, round shaped open instruments and asked if I had sexual relations before while inserting it inside of me, uncaring about my scream.

"Don't behave stupid and start to dress yourself," the sister said while I was still crying, ashamed and humiliated by the act done to my body, the violent test on my innocence, the test for the only reason to decide my future stay at one of the stations at Forest Home plus to inform about my personality and former lifestyle. I wondered the most if I still had my innocence, my pride, my virginity I had saved so far and only willing to give to the man I loved.

My question became answered by the last word the doctor spoke to the sister before I had left the room: still a Virgin.

Before the door became closed behind me, I was told to wait for a sister outside the doctor's office in order to become escorted back to the work room. I was hurt, physically and mentally, unable to face the sister or the girls after I carefully set down on my chair with my blushing face pointed to the ground. Some girls started to giggle and became instantly stopped by the authorial voice of one of the sisters on duty.

The day never seemed to end, still for the first time at Forest Home I was thankful for not having to talk to anyone. Finally, I found my privacy inside my tiny room, isolated from reality, alone with my thoughts and feelings, separated from my boyfriend and longing for my grandfather. The more I thought about him and asked for his help, my desperate need for relief became answered by the flow of my tears which never seemed to end that very evening. Before I fell asleep that night I thought about how great it would be to have some writing paper and a pencil, a chance to collect my thoughts and feelings by writing a daily journal.

The next morning during work, I was slipped a tiny piece of paper by the girl placed at the chair next to me during a brief moment the sister had turned her head. I was curious about the meaning and had to wait for my turn to use the bathroom at lunch time before I was able to decipher its written contents on a small white portion torn from the newspaper piece used as toilette paper. The message was written by using the eye of a needle plus the blood from ones fingertip, the only way to communicate among each other.

I was surprised how someone could come up with such answer to one of the forbidden rules of Forest Home before I realized the dirty contents depicted on the paper: "Ich hätte auch gern mal wieder meine Beine breitgemacht!" (I also would have loved to spread my legs again.) Again, here I was reminded of the humiliating action from the day before and had lost my appetite for lunch. One had to finish whatever was put on the plate in order to avoid punishment, and that day it took forever to eat my portion.

I was upset about such nasty remark and took it very personal before I had to learn that the group was dominated by several bullies who tried to intimidate the rest of us. Some of them had been at Forest Home for a long period of time, kind of being part of the inventory. Some others had gained the sister's trust and report certain controversial action from individuals or within the group; in simple words, we had snitches among us.

The first couple of weeks at the reception station I became occupied by several different handcrafts like mending socks or put handmade button holes into sewn duvet and pillowcases. Within a short period of time my already marked mind by my father's authority of achieving perfect results in any taken project, became topped by utter perfection due to the thread of punishment or being confronted in front of the group. Very often ones handcrafted results became torn apart with the request to start all over again.

Knowing already how to knit, I had to prove my ability by knitting my own monthly sanitary napkins out of white, thick cotton thread, altogether eight pieces and due to its thickness almost impossible to use. All personal napkins had to be provided with each personal number, in my case number 830.

To me it was just another humiliating action, but most of all I felt sorry for the girl on duty who had to collect each day all used bloody napkins from all stations to dump them into a huge kettle filled with water and powdered soap in order to bring the contents to a boil and steer the bloody mess. This course had to be repeated several times before all napkins seemed to be clean, all white before rinsed in cold water. At first they became drained off by hand before totally drained by a centrifuge, then dried by a huge dryer and sorted out by numbers.

Each month I was afraid days before it was time for my period, knowing I had to wear such uncomfortable, unsanitary hand knitted napkins which would bulk up my underwear and make it almost impossible to sit on a chair for an entire day without chafing ones private parts. Somehow I was very lucky for never having to perform the nastiest job at Forest Home.

On Sunday morning all individual stations would gather and walk in perfect formation down the hill toward the small local church to take part at Sundays mess. To be a newcomer at Forest Home, one was excluded for several weeks to participate, out of fear one could escape.

When I was permitted to come along I was glad to leave Forest Home behind, even though for only a few hours, the chance to see some normal people for a short while. Sundays was the only time one was permitted to exchange the wooden shoes for one's personal ones for going to church. However, I always could notice several girls who had to wear their wooden shoes as punishment for failing certain rules, including myself several times.

When we had arrived at the small but beautiful church, several local boys had gathered in front and insulted us with nasty remarks, making me blush. This was another humiliating moment I knew I would have to face each Sunday while attending church, and I was afraid and embarrassed about recurring happenings.

Once a month, on Sunday afternoon we were given one piece of paper plus a pencil in order to write a letter to our parents. It took a while before I learned how to write the perfect letter that would pass the censure by Mother Superior and not be held without ever being mailed. At first I had mentioned about the reality, dos and don'ts at Forest Home, releasing my hurt and frustration in an accusatory way by revolting against the lies I was told about Forest Home, the betrayal on my person.

Soon I figured that it might be smarter to lie about the happenings and paint a positive picture about what was going on behind the walls of Forest Home. Actually, it did not make any difference, except the more relaxing attitude the sisters showed towards me, my parents never answered any of my letters or sent anything like a small parcel, some girls were able to receive at Christmas plus their birthdays.

After several months without ever receiving any mail from my parents or Wulf, I thought it would be useless to send more letters without ever getting an answer, however I was forced to continue, consequently left with hopes never to be satisfied, tormenting my mind in sleepless nights.

During such nights I often thought about my past and ended up either thinking about grandpa or Wulf. I did not know if Wulf had written letters which never became forwarded, nor if he had given up on his girlfriend who probably was not suitable for him anymore. All unanswered questions turned into physical pain with the only relief by talking to my grandfather. Just talking to him made me calm, gave me strength to face another day at Forest Home.

I thought about the first time I ever consciously saw grandpa who had been given a ride in his neighbor's car to visit us, delivering goods from the farm. He had called me "Heikelein" for the very first time while lifting me up close to his face where I got tickled by his thick reddish moustache, his personal pride.

Years later at visits to the farm, I always got excited by watching him taking care of it by cutting and grooming it, twirling the ends between his fingers to make them stand upright. Grandpa still was considered a handsome man in his second part of life. His hair was almost white and cut short. It almost seemed impossible to decide whether his freckled face decorated by the reddish grown moustache, or his green eyes were the focal point of his radiant external characteristic.

How could I ever forget sitting on his knees while listening to all the exciting stories about America, the country of freedom and prosperity, the land of milk and honey and possibilities for everyone. Yes, I was longing for freedom and good food, the food I remembered being spoiled with at my grandparents' farm.

I already talked about our servings for breakfast and have to talk about the everyday meals, as well. Our lunch and supper consisted mostly of carbohydrates, like potatoes, pancakes, hardy soups made from barley lacking protein, or thick oatmeal soups cooked with water. There never was any meat or fruit at the table except on Christmas or Easter holidays, and the only salads I remember were fixed from dandelions, sorrel or stinging nettle we had to pick ourselves.

No wonder that all the girls started to look healthy by the shape of their bodies, except their pale faces could not hide the lack of nourishment. We all had gained weight, almost by the week, sitting on a chair for more than eight hours a day without a chance of exercise, except the short mutual walk every day after lunch without the permission to communicate among us girls.

Sometimes one was asked the join the sister who lead the way, or to walk with the one behind the group, a lucky day for those who were given the chance to talk. At evenings, after the door had been closed behind me, I started to exercise inside my room after I had studied the part of the Bible ordered by Mother Superior. Once a month we all had to step onto the scale in order to compare our weight from the month before, to make sure that each individual gained some weight for a satisfying notice to be added to our personal documents, a proof to the authorities that one's condition had improved, if only by one's physical looks.

Within three years, during my stay at Forest Home I still had gained about thirty pounds in addition to my daily exercises.

Every week we became challenged by "Fleisskaertchen", a bonus of thirty cents if we had managed to reach our required workload. Dropping a pair of scissors, or falling back on the daily work require-ment, each time a dime would be taken off the weekly bonus, and the chance for buying an apple or some sweets was gone.

Once I had accumulated enough money to buy a perfumed piece of soap, reminiscing for days about the time when Wulf had pleased me with a piece of lavender soap during my first and only visit to him.

To think about Wulf and our mutual individual hurt about the illness of both our mothers had always intensified the need to be close to each other, giving us the feeling to be loved. Here I was stripped of everything I had called my own and I really felt sorry for myself. For the first time I experienced the hurt with its resulting agony of being locked up, deprived of everything, being treated worse than a convict.

Within the first few weeks at Forest Home I had developed claustrophobia, an illness that would accompany me throughout my entire life.

Before I became transferred to the "Baby Station", located in the main building where young girls or those still considered being a virgin were under the guidance of the sister second in line to Mother Superior, I was taught all different handcrafts needed to produce items sold at the annual bazaar held at Forest Home.

It was considered a privilege to become chosen for the Baby or House station, to be part of thirty young girls selected by their individual non-sexual or less sexual background, with a good chance to become totally reformed to a perfect citizen we were told.

Actually, nothing bad changed. My room looked similar to the one I had occupied for the first six month, furnished with a single iron bed, a console, a metal wash bowl and a chair, the crucifix above my bed, the iron bars in front of my window plus the missing door handle inside, even my bedspread, pillow and towel were sewn from the same fabric. To grow up in a tiny apartment were the kitchen with the old sofa had been my bedroom. At night I still was able to create my personal need for beauty by picking wild flowers in order to please my parents and to satisfy myself.

Forest Home with its deprivation of personal belongings had intensified my hunger for beauty with no chance for fulfillment except in my own imagination and during walks to church on Sunday mornings. I could not wait to inhale the intensive aroma released by the pine trees along the way, and for a little while I was part of nature, feeling free before the local boys gathering at the church entrance brought me back to reality.

Forest Home had its own seating arrangement inside the church, at the very back right side, close to the entry door where passing church goers always took a glance at us, revealing their thoughts with discriminating looks, a recurring reminder of my status, being a bad girl.

Each time I caught such expression toward my direction, I had to concentrate for not screaming out loudly, reminding myself to keep quiet, to swallow my anger in order to avoid consequences.

Today I am still not quite sure how I managed to keep my self-confidence during such influences of on-going discriminations by the sisters plus the public. How can one survive at a young age when told over and over again to be bad, to be worthless and to be a fallen girl. It is quite understandable that due to such negative suggestions, eighty per cent of all the girls once being held at Forest Home had no chance after being released back into society where they failed, consequently being returned to Forest Home until the age of 21.

At the Baby Station I was one of the older girls seated in a chair along the wall in a circle knitting socks for German soldiers who were part of the Bundeswehr (German Army). Again we were watched and observed by two sisters sitting opposite each other at an oval table in the middle of the room. Day after day I performed the same duty and routine for about six month.

At the beginning I had to count stitches distributed among four needles while learning to knit socks. Later on I started to count days, thinking about where life might take me in my future years after having reached the age of 21, the magical number providing freedom, the freedom of being an adult, able to decide and take responsibility for one's own person. Here I was sixteen years of age, still five long years apart from freedom, thinking about digits which might influence my future life, digits involving the past, present and future.

When unable to communicate, one learns to observe in a more sensitive way the people around, in my case the girls in my visual range within the circle. I learned how to interpret their body language, reading the silent message in their eyes about the same needs. We all wanted someone to open up to, someone to listen to our personal problems, someone who would understand and not blame us for whatever gave the reason for being locked up and treated worse than a prisoner.

Since there was nobody who offered such kindness, my only comfort was the knowledge for not having to suffer alone, for being one of many who shared the same treatment for becoming reformed to face and fit into society. Night after night I relived my beautiful and positive memories from my youth in the solitary of my dark room in order to keep my sanity and gain strength, not to give up like some of the girls before me who had found their peace at one corner of the local cemetery, belonging to Forest Home.

Somehow I lived a double life in order to survive. To the outside I appeared like an obedient, however considered difficult girl who needed special guidance. At the inside I was a volcano, ready to explode any single day, consumed by my thoughts about the unfairness that had haunted my life, starting with childhood. Maybe I just waited for that special moment to unleash my feelings inside, the chance to rebel against the entire system. Well, I got my chance, offering the relief needed for not getting mad, a relief I had to trade with six weeks of solitary confinement.

One of the girls was denied to use the bathroom during work time and did wet her pants. At once she received an outraged verbal discrimination by one of the sisters and was told to sit on her chair until evening without the chance of changing cloth. The "Butze", a tiny room within the attic and distanced from anything that could remind of time or daily routine, was the place where one had to think, about ones disobediences, failing the rules of Forest Home, the place to research one's own conscience and soul, the place for solitary confinement. It was the tiniest room so far, crowded by an iron bed, chair, iron wash bowl, chamber pot, plus the most important item, the Bible. The towel and bedding always became removed after breakfast and returned after supper. There was nothing to do, no chance for lying down during the day, the only thing to do was to read the Bible.

I did not mind studying the Holy Book about the teachings of our Lord, the challenge on our soul to make the right decision between Good and Evil, plus adapting the promise of forgiveness to anyone who believes in his Word.

To be locked up without the chance of communicating with anyone was hard so far. To be disconnected from visual human contact was the hardest part. My mid got raped by the most crazy ideas about what was right or wrong, whom to blame and how to manage to escape. But where could I run to?

My father had contacted the youth welfare department and consequently turned over his parental authority. My mother was ill and depending on my father and physician in order to survive, one day at a time. Grandfather and grandmother had gone to a better place, plus my sister was still a stranger to me.

This time it was a different situation, my will to believe was questioned by circumstances and influenced by persons who bad no qualified educational background for taken care of "fallen girls", their qualification was their strong faith, a free ticket for judgement and punishment? All this might sound controversial to the people who might read my story, who even might be offended by my thoughts because of their personal strong beliefs.

If one has to face a desperate situation, one comes up with thoughts unknown to oneself by trying to find the end of the tunnel. Each morning I woke up by the rattle of the sister's key chain while she was climbing up the steep stairs leading to the attic. And each morning, before the key had unlocked my door, I had to convince myself that I was not a bad person in order to make it through the day.

To be in solitary confinement meant to get used to a different routine. The door became opened by the sister on duty whose mimic became a daily reminder to my situation. The tray with my food always was carried by a different girl each day whose face revealed the same compassion like all the others before her. Even the tough ones who sometimes had to prove their power showed their sympathy towards my suffering.

Well, I had dared to rebel against the cruel rules of Forest Home by jumping out of my chair in order to oppose with a loud voice the cruel and embarrassing treatment by one of the sister to the girl who had wet her pants. With my behavior and daring action of rebelling in front of everybody, my status within the group had changed, and I received several notes from girls who complimented me to my outburst.

Like I mentioned before, those notes were all written with the eye of a needle, using one's personal blood as needed ink for depicting messages on the blank edge of a newspaper, cut to be used as toilet paper. The tray carrying my food always became controlled by the sister before it was placed on my chair, the moment the message was hidden below it. Each day I looked forward to such seemingly trivial expressions as my comfort which desperately I needed and appreciated each new day.

The exchange of notes became a game, a new excitement needed to keep my eagerness to oppose the regime, a simple tool to protect my-self from giving up like some of the girls who did not care anymore about themselves or their future. I still cared about myself and some-how knew that sadly I had the need to convince people with my per-sonal values, to prove, that deep inside I was a good person.

While days turned into weeks, my thoughts about my past helped to look forward to my unknown future in hope for better days. Where would I be in ten or twenty years, or even at the age of forty? I only knew that time was on my side, however patience never had been my strongest virtue. At Forest Home we were forced to be patient with-out asking questions, consequently being left within our own silence and quest for answers. My imaginative thoughts flourished due to lack of communication and personal contact, a profit to my future development of artistic endeavor.

Finally, I was released back into the group with the knowledge that solitary confinement did not break my spirit. Silence and isolation had enhanced my ability to extend my thinking to a certain balance where peace and contentment battled with the rage of rebellion, an opportunity to be used either way.

I wondered how I might react when faced with a similar situation? Would the knowledge of possible punishment hinder my inner uprising in fear of isolation? Yes, I was afraid of being locked up inside a tiny room with a missing door handle and a barred window. Yes, I was scared of the rattling sound of a key chain close or distant to me. And yes, I was mostly scared of loosing my mind. To be back among the other girls was a momentary relief, and I noticed a few more smiles in my direction, a good feeling compared to the vigilant eyes of the sisters. Nothing had changed except my work order, I was placed behind a sewing machine to learn the trade that would influence my future life at a time when I was a single mother, responsible to take care plus support two teenage boys, being the only bread winner.

At first I had to learn how to operate an industrial machine, different in speed from the one in school when I was challenged to combine constant rhythmical peddling with seemingly straight stitching to the eye. Soon I was able to tame the motor with the right feeling needed to operate individually to the project.

Forest Home was manufacturing gloves for the German military, and I was one of half a dozen girls who tried hard to reach their daily requirement of eighteen pair, thirty-six gloves a day.

Each glove had to be flawless and controlled for perfection by a sister who would decide if it would end up back on my table or added to the ones already piled up under my number 830 to be counted at the end of the day. It was a hard job with no chance of mental peace, a constant pressure from fear of failing the requested work leading to punishment or the loss of the weekly thirty cents.

Behind the machine I was alone with my thoughts and myself, unable to observe the girls within the circle. Our sewing machines were placed in ninety degree to the wall with just enough distance to each other for the chair, changing the formation within the room closer to the sister's desk. Sometimes I couldn't resist to look around, hoping that the silent motor would not give me away.

For about six month I was placed behind the machine, until the day when I was asked to see Mother Superior. The interruption of daily routine plus to see Mother Superior automatically questioned my conscience. What had I done this time? No matter how I felt about myself or unable to recall recent failure, I always carried a guilty conscience.

To be called by Mother Superior in general meant something unusual or bad or might happen; in my case it was an opportunity of one day of freedom, one day away from Forest Home, the chance of visiting my mother who had undergone brain surgery and had been transferred to an asylum.

For a moment I was blocked by the dull hurt inside my stomach, unable to move or control my tears, totally overwhelmed by the chance of freedom, the freedom of one day away from Forest Home, and hopefully with an opportunity to contact Wulf.

Mental Institution

After the entrance door and the gate to Forest Home were locked behind me, I actually believed that I was free, confirmed by the incredible adrenalin rush overtaking my entire body, revitalizing my senses. Knowing about the limitation of my freedom did not change my happiness, I would have been happy just for the chance of being away from Forest Home for only one hour.

This time I did not look back after I set down next to the same social worker in the back of the same car that had brought me to Forest Home, seemingly an eternity ago, too afraid Mother Superior could change her mind about my leaving.

I still was upset about all the lies I was told before, but did not dare to confront the woman next to me, the one who had all the power to determine my destiny, to keep quiet would be smarter than to interfere with my luck. Shortly after I was brought to Forest Home, mother had been taken to a hospital in a major city, not too far away from my hometown, to be observed and prepared for an operation, for brain surgery, related to the presumption of a tumor triggering her epileptically attacks. Due to an unfortunate outcome she became transferred to a mental institution where she had been since, paralyzed at the right side of her body, isolated from the public among other human beings who had lost part or total capacity of their mental function.

Thinking about my mother brought up the guilt of never having been really close to her, instead of trying to please her, all I cared was to get the attention of my father in hope to receive something back, anything positive, may be some love?

Now, I finally understood why I had to leave home, my father already had known then about the upcoming surgery of my mother and wanted to get rid of me as well, to be out of his way.

To realize the truth combined with all of my false hope for caring, finally helped to ease my needs for love or attention coming from my father. That moment I was cured, unafraid of hurt and convinced I did not care about him anymore.

My thoughts about my mother often got interrupted by my excitement for the chance to contact Wulf. What had happened to him? Was he still at the same university? How could I find out? I knew that his parents already had a telephone, but did I dare to ask for Wulf, afraid of becoming discriminated for the second time? The mental institution with its barred windows also was protected by a rod iron fence, reminding me of Forest Home. With the social worker at my side I waited for the door to become unlocked, unaware and uncertain about the next few hours.

Someone was on its way to the entry door with that dreaded sound of a rattling key chain, so familiar to me, and all of a sudden I had another encounter with a sister wearing the same habit like all the others at Forest Home. Later I found out that the mental institution was operated by sisters belonging to the same holy order like the ones in Forest Home.

This time I was greeted in a friendly, not patronizing way by a young sister, consequently calming the instant resentment inside of me.

"You must be Caroline's daughter," the sister said, "your mother is already waiting for you."

No one had prepared me for the moment I saw my mother after months that had changed both of our lives. She always had appeared in my memory as the simple, yet attractive woman before she had to live with her epileptic attacks.

The person occupying the bed did not resemble the one I had kept in my mind. This person could not be my mother. Everything about her former appearance had changed into the opposite.

Her face was swollen and her body had expanded enormously due to medication and lacking movements. A scarf was wrapped around her head, hiding the huge scar, the sad reminder of undergoing torture by opening mother's scull with hammer and chisel for surgery without being given total anesthesia. She had been deadening with local anesthesia, her hand and feet tied up by leather belts to the operation table, a piece of wood kept between her teeth to bite on, a necessarily prevention for biting her tong while screaming.

I don't think no one could ever imagine the pain she had to endure during such inhuman torture.

She had survived the operation, confused, with right side of her body being paralyzed.

Mother had lived with her illness over several years, undetected and falsely medicated by our doctor who finally changed his diagnose from menopause to brain tumor. By then the medical insurance refused coverage for an operation, cancelling my mother's membership with the advice to agree to experimental surgery, meaning, being used as a guinea pig for brain surgery.

This was the last straw, the chance for ending her tormenting headaches plus repeated epileptical attacks. My parents agreed, and my mother became one of the first patients ever operated on brain tumor, at a time when such crucial surgery still was at the initial state of scientific research in Germany, at the beginning of 1960.

Confronted with the most sad encounter I never could have imagined before, I instantly experienced pitiful emotions. I thought about the good times we had together, trying to convert pitiful feelings into sympathy. How happy mother was, when in my younger age I had taken the bike plus an empty burlap sack in order to collect fallen apples during fall at an orchard a few miles away from home. A previous storm that helped to fill the entire sack, and consequently made me push my bike, trying to keep the precious load balanced on top the rod connecting saddle and steering wheel.

My mother already was waiting at home with all the jars, already sterilized and placed neatly on top clean cotton cloths at the kitchen table, ready to be filled with fresh apple given by nature and processed into the most delicious dessert. That very day she run out of jars and tried to save the undamaged ones by placing them on top the same shelf lined with old newspapers that showed off the effort of both of our labor. The shelf had its place downstairs in the basement, next to the bricks of coal neatly piled up in one corner of a small cellar.

Mother was delighted and pleased about all the apples I had collected and asked me to help to peel, handing me one of the two metal plus a peeling knife, given to her by grandmother. As much as I tried to copy my mother by trying to end up with one undamaged peel from an apple, I never succeeded, always admiring her for such artistic handwork.

There also were those already harvested potato fields still hiding overlooked earth apples, scattered undetected amongst dug up soil which I proudly collected in contemplation of praise from both of my parents.

I fondly remembered the time I had begged my mother for a quarter, in order to fulfill a long time desire to rent one of the first scooters equipped with real balloon tires. Mother made it happen, and I never forgot the time I proudly spent a couple of hours trying to gain high speed with help of my right foot pushing, riding around the neighborhood in hope some of the kids would see me.

Sometimes I would accompany my father to the train station, to the track where wagons filled with coals became distributed to the occupying forces who would show up and fill their trucks up to the rim with the considered "black gold" during those hard times.

My father and myself always had to hide amongst the wagons, waiting for the moment when everybody had left and the two of us could collect the bricks of coal fallen down while being transferred from the wagons by shovel on to the trucks. We were not permitted to do so and had to take cover, afraid of being detected. To me it always was an adventure, being part of a forbidden action in the company of my father, but most of all I was proud to see my mother being happy about a few more coals which would contribute additional heat to-gether with the kindling firewood collected by my father and myself at the closest forest, always in fear to be caught by the forest ranger.

All those thoughts of gone by years rushed through my mind while looking at my mother, trying to ease my conscience by giving credit to all those positive moments I remembered, the few times when I really felt close to her. Now I was troubled by my feelings, I felt sorry for rejecting and blaming her during her years of undetected illness, in times she had pushed me away and could not stand having me around, when she had thrown things at me, or took me into the basement for a beating.

I was overcome by guilt, unable to verbalize my thoughts or anything that came to mind, I just stood there with my head down, unable to shed any tears, hoping she would sense my inner turmoil plus guilt with the instinct of a mother while looking at me. She did not talk, and I was not certain if she could recognize me.

My young mind was troubled more than before, questioning all the happenings that had influenced my entire life so far. Why was I being punished over and over again? The same question I had asked before and would ask for many more years to come.

I had lost track of time when the sister who had returned into the room, telling me I had to leave, it was time for mother's therapeutic exercises.

The social worker had waited in the hall way during my visit and escorted me back to the car. She kept quiet for a while until she answered my unspoken question: "What now?"

"We still have some time left before I have to take you back. Would you like to talk about your mother?" she asked.

She told the chauffeur to stop at the next café on the way to Forest Home to order a cup of coffee and to please me with a hot chocolate.

I could sense her different behavior and wondered if her change of heart had something to do with my mother's illness or if she suddenly started to feel sorry for me. My mind still had to digest the last few hours, confused with sadness about my mother, myself and the desire to talk to the person I loved the most.

I still don't know why I did not ask for a chance to contact Wulf by writing a few lines, explaining the unwritten letters plus my situation. I also forgot to ask why my letters to my parents never became answered. All I asked was how much more time I would have to spend at Forest Home.

That late afternoon I was told the second time that everything would depend entirely on my own behavior, when the sisters decided that I was ready to fit back into society.

My Father

To talk about my father is one of the hardest tasks. When I was a little girl, I looked up to him, like one looks up to one's hero. That was the time he gave me all of his attention if I followed his rules and was able to remember facts about his war stories during frequent session. He was a man with a mission, reliving his war memories by enforcing them on me with strictness and imponderable mood swings.

He treated me as a boy with the expectation of disciplinary behavior and strength. His expectations were high, and if I did not excel to his wants, he shunned me by withdrawing his attention or reacted with uncontrollable rage that often degenerated in physical punishment. To me his withdrawal of attention was equal to withdrawal of love, a reason for feeling guilty.

My upbringing involved lots of situations where guilt troubled my conscience for not obeying certain rules set by my father. As an adult I tried to fight set rules by running against the wind, still losing due to a conscious mind.

My father was born into German aristocracy by the genealogical tree on his mother's side, who had married a war hero of the "Great War" who was not of aristocrat descent but remembered by his legacy that a small village had taken his name. My father's parents died in an accident when he was a small boy, and for a while he lived with his grandmother who taught him the proper rules and behavior of the upper class. After her death he was brought into an orphanage, where he stayed until he turned six.

A local farmer with lots of land and already several children took him in, using him as a farm hand and made him sleep in the barn. Came spring, my father had to walk barefoot, including to school, until fall arrived.

During meals, he had to stand at the table and was not allowed to start eating until the farmer started, and had to finish the same time the farmer put down his eating utensils. In his early youth he learned to follow orders and to act in a disciplinary way. He grew up without love or attention.

When I think about his upbringing I do understand his behavior towards me, he just did not know better. I guess, this means an explanation of a "Devil's Circle". Besides his hard work of long hours on the farm, he excelled at school, and when he became of age ready to learn a trade, the local parson tried to convince him to follow in his footsteps.

All that my father wanted to do is to widen his horizon, to learn things, and show the world that he could achieve anything he had set his mind on. He was bitter about his upbringing, but never forgot the teaching of his grandmother that he had blue blood running through his veins, that he was part of the "Aryan Race".

When I started to write about my father, I was torn between my moral responsibility that one should "Love thy Parents" and not talk ill about the dead. The knowledge of the atrocity committed by "Hitler's Elite" against the Jewish Race had not changed my father's behavior nor elitist attitude connected with the doctrines of the Third Reich. He was unwilling to accept guilt about having been one of Hitler's Puppets.

There was no hate inside of me, only contempt for the man who was my father, who had inflicted his beliefs into my mind and had tried with all of his might to create his little "Tin Soldier" who could remember and hand down his legacy to the next generation.

I had to take some time off to clear my mind, to find the right answer for my personal reason to hand down my memories admitting my father's wrongdoing and thinking. All of my life I had tried to distant myself from the past, trying to forget his influential power that had troubled my conscience and hindered to rid myself from the burden on my shoulders.

I tried hard to receive my freedom of mind but did not succeed. There must be a truth about the saying, that generations still being punished for the sins of their fathers. To write about my past might be the answer to my request for relief and maybe other women who might have experienced a similar upbringing, were embarrassed or ashamed to talk about it.

During the 50s and the 60s, the adult children of the "Front generation" accused their own fathers without ever receiving a response. The former soldiers never admitted their guilt nor opened up to their experiences that had marked their lives. Their needed justification became the "Nazi Ideology of Race" and the children who had to endure the degenerated souls of their fathers were too ashamed and embarrassed to talk about it.

I am thinking about my sister who managed to carry her burden by simple denial. Whenever I tried to talk about my father, she just changed the subject. My sister never really experienced the attention of a father, and when she and I became exchanged during summer vacation, she managed not to be seen with my father, even though she had no idea about his past.

She probably could sense the aversion my father subconsciously had towards her and my mother, by telling both about their lack of intelligence. That also explains her aversion towards me during our upbringing. Even though we seldom saw each other she knew about our father's affinity toward her younger sister.

During summer vacation I was sent to my grandparents and my sister to the city. She did not speak the proper High German language and was ashamed around other city children who often made fun of her strange dialect. She took everything to heart, bottled up her anger and lived an introverted life, always denying her parents and her little sister, myself. The two of us were absolute the opposite from each other and it took many years of our lives before we had any close relationship.

There still is not an intimate bond between the two of us, but we are able to communicate without blame and show our fondness. Sometimes I get confused when she talks about "our mother" not meaning our mutual one, but her mother-in-law with whom she shared her entire life under one roof, still living near the small little village she grew up in, communicating with her family and neighbors in the same old German dialect spoken since people had settled in that particular part of Northern Germany.

My sister needed the security of a family and was not keen on exploring beyond her surroundings. Sometimes I think about how we must have felt about each other while growing up. She was jealous about my High German speaking and my tomboyish attitude. My jealousy towards her resulted from her growing up on the farm, for not having to wear second-hand clothing.

After my father had finished school, he left the small villa and started an apprenticeship at a German newspaper in Northern Germany. He was starving for knowledge and recognition. He already knew that discipline is equal to power and patience the road to success. His upbringing and youth without ever having any possession had helped him to develop a great imagination, and his growing self-assurance enabled him to charm his superior with intelligence and manners combined with disciplinary behavior.

He was eager to be someone, and slowly but surely climbed the corporate ladder. He became a successful addition to the team. Over years, the memory of his upbringing had never left his mind, still lingering, reminding him of his grandmother, telling him to be of aristocracy descent and therefore a special person.

Being influenced over years and daily exposed to the propaganda of the NSDAP printed by his newspaper, he willingly supported more and more the beliefs of the Nazi Party. Himmler's goal was to change the "Waffen-SS" to an elite of Aryan "Herrenmenschen" after he was named the new "SS-Reichsfuehrer". Even though my father already had achieved his goal to be successful, Himmler's new Waffen-SS was the challenge he had waited for his entire life, to be one of the selected and elite group of men who fervently believed in a new "Arische Ordnung" (Aryan order). This was his chance to be one of the chosen one, he applied with the "Waffen-SS".

After my father had married my mother, he kept his apartment close to work, visiting my mother frequently who decided to stay on the farm with her family during her pregnancy. My mother, a beautiful tall woman with gold blond hair and green eyes represented the image of Hitler's imagination about the perfect Aryan woman, the most important reason of my father's commitment, another factor, the desire of having a son.

Shortly after my sister was born, my father applied with the "Waffen-SS". All applicants with the desire to belong to the ideological elite unit had to represent the ideal of the perfect German race, to be of Aryan descent and without ever being accused of any crime. Potential recruits had to be tall, in perfect physical health and give absolute dedication to the Fuehrer Adolf Hitler, even to sacrifice their own lives for him.

The training was given in camps of individual SS regiments, close to each soldier city of birth. Instructors emphasized that the SS soldier belonged to the circle of the "chosen People". Aggressiveness and perfection in combat was their objective. Men would be forced to the edge of their load bearing capacity. Lectures were held about the principle of the NSDAP and SS philosophy and theories about their racial superiority opposite the Slav and Jews who were considered being "Untermenschen".

The entire training also contained the drill of using and assembling their shotgun. Extended marching and hours of exercises made sure that each SS man was in perfect physical condition. Every third recruit failed training the first time. If one did complete, the candidate was sent to one of the SS infantry or cavalry schools, before he swore his oath of unshaken obedience to the Fuehrer.

The recruitment was finished and the former, sometimes ordinary man had been changed into a fanatic elite warrior who followed unconditionally every command, even if forced the termination of prisoners of war and cruelty towards civilians. The brainwashing had degraded and stripped the finished soldier of his identity, subsidizing his morals for the fanatic doctrine of the "Waffen-SS".

After writing about the process of training future SS warriors, I am unable to find an excuse to justify my father. I have to admit that hate never had reached my heart, only deep contempt, the last barrier before hate, enough to save myself from guilt. A feeling controlled deep in our hearts and souls by the "Ten Commandments" telling us to love and honor our parents. I wish I would be able to loose the anger for being a Nazi's child, brainwashed by my father with the same Nazi doctrines and prejudice towards the Jewish race, carrying my load for the rest of my life.

Many important memories go back to my early years, the time my father tried to force his belief and conviction into my young mind by giving me the same brainwashing he once received. He made and called me his "Little Tin Soldier". His emphasis of teaching me to be strong, tough and intelligent, better than anybody else was based on his pride that even his lost war had not evaporated from his mind: We both belonged to the superior race, exceptional people with the obligation to excel. In order to force this challenge upon a little girl's brain, his words became emphasized by exciting and colorful stories reliving his war as a hero, unforgettable to a little girl's mind who was too young to judge but believed the man who showed attention, an attention that often involved severe physical punishment unleashed from uncontrollable rage.

I often think about little girls who had a chance to play with dolls and sit on their daddy's lab, given unconditional love and understanding. I think about little girls growing up to become teenagers, waiting for their first date and dreaming of their first kiss. The opportunity was never given to me, in a sense, my youth was taken away and I became deprived of childhood and my teenage years.

The only time without fear I experienced on the farm with my grandparents where quietness and affection gave me peace of mind for a little while until the death of my grandfather.

Due to my father's upbringing in poverty, he never had the chance for higher education or to become an officer. To him his intelligence was all he needed to be successful and to make a name for himself. I wish I could remember all the details of his service record, the names of the medals and decoration given to him, but this story is about the struggle of a little girl, not about a false hero. Whenever I needed attention, I asked to be shown his "Iron Cross" and the story when "Uncle Adolf " personally had bestowed it upon him.

Father was more than pleased to open up and it seemed that his entire personality had changed for a while. In his euphoria he always pointed out that his middle name was Adolf, and looking back to such moments I believe his identification was more than just with his name.

Moments like those changed him into a different person who still believed in the "Superior Race" his "Fatherland" and beloved "Fuehrer". With emphasis he always pointed out that he had fought on all fronts during the war, assigned to a special outfit, being part of the "Blitzkrieg", fighting the partisans in Poland and having been with several divisions Counter Intelligence, Air Force, division "Reich" and "Wehrmacht".

There was this photo I never forgot. I guess it was taken in Rumania where soldiers with pointed guns made gypsies dance on the railroad track. My father was posing in the background with several soldiers in front of a "JU 52" air plane, he was the only one without wearing a uniform. In a short distance a few generals had gathered in circle, and he told me all their names which I forgot over time.

I always remembered the air plane and his proud attitude while bragging about his flight with "Hanna Reitsch", Germany's first female pilot. That must have been one of his highlights and privilege of a special assignment. Hanna Reitsch became my role model and from that time on I wanted to become a pilot to please my father.

My Mother

She was born in a small village in the year 1914 as the youngest of four siblings. The oldest brother had drowned in his youth, and grandma was alone with three children when grandfather had to go to war. It was a small farming-village, and probably not more than 500 people living close to each other, trading and exchanging their handy work for goods and food. It was a community of farmers, some with more land or property than others, and some with only a few animals for their personal use.

My grandparents owned a few pigs, some chickens and ducks. Friederich, my grandfather, was an artist, weaving baskets, and carving our wooden shoes. Besides taking care of the forest as a ranger, he was considered being the best butcher in the village. Once a week plus Sundays he volunteered his time to the local church, being their servant.

My grandparents never had a surplus of money in their possession, but there was always enough to eat, but most of all Love between them and their grandchildren. In all those years I had known them, I never heard them exchanging strong words.

I guess, my mother grew up in peaceful and simple surroundings, learning all the chores a young girl at that particular time in life had to know. She was part of a community where farm children received a simple education taught in the old German dialect. She never had a chance for a higher education, the privilege of rich city children. My mother turned out to be an attractive young woman with golden blond hair and green eyes. When she became about 20 years of age, she left the small village to take a job as a maid with a wealthy family in Southern Germany, where she stayed until she met my father.

I knew my parents had met when mother came home to celebrate Thanksgiving with her parents. It always was a big feast when locals and visitors socialized inside a huge tent enjoying the music of the small band while drinking beer and observing some strangers who especially had come to dance.

Outside the tent one could admire the wagons decorated with flowers and garlands of grain to enhance to purpose of its load, a generous combination of harvested fruit of the land to be given to the less fortunate.

Most of the visitors were young men drawn by the chance of dancing and maybe to meet someone. My father was one of them to be part of the celebration. During that time he was working as an editor of a newspaper in a larger town, located not too far from my grand-parents' village. I guess my father was drawn to my mother's physical appearance. In his mind her blond hair and green eyes represented the picture of Hitler's ideal about the perfect woman, the incarnation of the Aryan Race.

My mother was drawn by the handsome stature and good looks of my father who seemed to be so different from the young men she had known from the village. She was charmed by his appearance as well as knowledge and intrigued by his occupation. They had met several times more before mother had ended her vacation.

Shortly after being back at work my mother realized being pregnant with my older sister. My father took the responsibility and proposed marriage, to him a consequent act due to his still honorable and moral conviction at that time. Shortly after my sister was born, my father decided to be an applicant with the Waffen-SS and became a soldier.

For a while my mother stayed at her parents' home, nursing and taking care of my sister. World War II had started and women were needed for work at a large ammunition factory located about 30 miles south of my grandparents' village. My mother left my sister with my aunt and grandparents and moved to the city. She rented a tiny apartment upstairs at the home of an elderly couple close to the ammunition factory. Her days were filled with long hours including weekends, not enough time left for visits to the far.

Once in a while my father was able to come home. After one of his so called honorably acquired "leaves" in 1942, my mother became pregnant with her second child. Nine month later I was born.

Since my mother was busy due to long working hours and required overtime on weekends, our landlady took care of me during the day.

The first common bond with my mother that comes to memory was the time we had to stand in line for hours waiting to receive our weekly stamps which we needed for buying food. I also remember the sirens alarming us to take cover and move if possible to the next shelter before enemy planes had reached our city and dropped their devastating bombs. I guess we could call ourselves lucky, neither the house we lived in, nor the factory my mother worked at had ever been hit.

As long the two of us were together, I saw my mother in the evenings after she had returned from work. Most of the time she was exhausted and did not have the energy to give her full attention or to play with me.

My father was missing in action, decent food was unavailable and my mother was stressed by fear during work time that the factory might be hit by a bomb.

As an adult I did understand her struggle combined with loneliness, enough excuse for me to feel for her. When I was small, she felt like a stranger to me, and it even escalated after my father had returned from imprisonment in Siberia.

Having her husband back did not mean that she was being released from her struggle or worries, now she had to support the three of us, since there was no work available for a former editor of a "Nazi Newspaper".

We moved out of the tiny apartment into a different place, this time my parents rented two rooms upstairs in a small house, located at the outskirts of town, close to wheat fields and farmland. Our landlady was a nice lady of aristocracy status, a war hero's widow. She shared the downstairs with her divorced daughter to whom I became very attached. Lots of times she had come to my rescue when my father had unleashed his uncontrolled anger by beating the hell out of me.

My father had changed during the war, adapting the doctrines and beliefs of the "Waffen-SS", by dedicating his entire being to his beloved Fuehrer Adolf Hitler, acting as his obedient puppet. He had become a different person. I never knew him like my mother did before the war but there were times I wished I had.

The apartment consisted of two rooms, a kitchen and a small bedroom. There also was a tiny pantry outside the kitchen door where mother could store some can goods, cleaning supplies and dirty laundry. We did not have a bathroom or toilet, only an earth closet located downstairs (a kind of outhouse) across the pig stable. One had to cross the wash-room with its huge wash boiler built into one corner and the metal-tub and wash-board next to it.

Since we did not have any wash facilities in our apartment, my mother had to carry the tub upstairs and fill it with hot water. It always took a while and many kettles filled with water being boiled on top the wood burning stove in our kitchen. This always happened on Saturday evenings and the three of us took turns. I always was the first to take a bath before I went to bed.

Up to my fifth year I shared my parents' bed, sleeping in the middle between them. After I had started elementary school, my bed became the old sofa in our kitchen. Besides the stove our kitchen was furnished with a cupboard, an old sofa, a tiny wash basin with a cold water faucet, a kitchen table with four chairs and next to the window a small round table with two chairs next to it. I still remember their woven seats with broad bands of denim, each covered with a hand sewn pillow by my mother.

When one entered the room, one could not oversee the enlarged black and white photograph placed at the wall above the small table, depicting my father in his black uniform. In my memory the picture always had dominated the entire room, releasing in me an ambivalent feeling of love and fear.

It is hard to think about our meager kitchen where nobody had a chance for privacy, the room without escape but dreaming for a little girl and probably for my mother as well. Every day she had to work, cleaning the house of a rich family at the other side of town.

During the day I either was alone or controlled by my father who started to pay extra attention to me, influencing my young mind to his liking, creating his little "Tin-Soldier". He always enforced his feelings about my mother on to me in a very negative way, talking about her weakness and lacking intelligence, creating a similar dislike in myself towards my mother and my sister whom he always mentioned in a negative connection with her. I believed everything he told me, finally somebody paid attention to me, more than I ever had received before.

During my early years I became detached from my mother and started to adore my father. There was another reason for my dislike towards her, she never could stand having me around when she was at home. She wanted me to go and play, and the only chance was the street.

Thinking back of growing up, nobody knew of her slowly developing illness since there were no obvious visible symptoms. Her only complain were recurring headaches my father did not take seriously. She did not dare to argue with him and rather kept any disagreement to herself out of fear for physical punishment and verbal abuse.

With time my father's frustration lead to a more violent behavior and I never forgot the day he made me stay while accusing my mother about her negligent appearance, pushing and slapping her around in his disgusting rage.

My mother never had a chance to take care of herself, she worked hard in order to make ends meet, trying to keep her family together without ever complaining. Sometimes she bought herself some chamomile tea for rinsing her washed hair. The only beauty treatment she ever used for herself.

Then came a day in my life that changed everything. One evening during supper she started to get this awkward look on her face, her entire body started to shake and she lost control and fell to the ground. Her entire body was overtaken by uncontrolled shaking, tong biting and a strange behavior that did not reveal a human being anymore.

My Mother Had Developed Brain Tumor

From now on frequent attacks followed and were related by our doctor with menopause. For a long time mother was being misdiagnosed and treated with the wrong medication. She had to stop working and we received welfare from the government.

My father was full of despise and felt sorry for himself, his heroic memories had tormented his brain since he had to face the new Germany after being released from imprisonment. His beloved country had to give in to foreign demands and he was unable to face defeat.

For many years he belittled the loss of the war by insisting his country only had ceasefire. He escaped his responsibility by not helping my mother with moral support or encouragement, his only compassion was connected to his own misery by feeling sorry for himself. He found a new interest and excuse for leaving the house to bet on horses. Even though there was no extra money to spare, he still went frequently to midtown where men of his age gathered in a small room to bet illegally on horse races.

There were times I had to fetch him because mother was in need of help. It took a while to get to midtown, and on my way I always got excited about the chance to receive a dime or even 50 Pfennig (Quarter) from someone who had just won some money. It had happened before.

The room was filled with smoke and verbally excited men, trying to make a buck and forget reality for a while. It always took a moment to find my father among the group that had crowded in front of the bookmaker's window, listening to the result of the last race announced from the radio, comparing their bets against the number of the horse that just had won the race. One had three chances to win money, the bet on the winning horse or the bet on first and second winner. The most money was made if one had bet on altogether, first, second and third winner in this sequence.

My father had figured out his own system, by comparing former races listed on a sheet at the bookmaker's window with predictions made by a racing magazine plus his own gut feeling. Sometimes he was able to select the first, second and third and made good money. After a couple of years he was banned by the bookmaker because of his winnings.

One day he told me, that after I had reached adulthood, he would pass his system on to me, but when the time came I had the strength to deny his inheritable weakness. During my teenage years mother's illness worsened and her incapacity had challenged my daily life. There were nights I did not dare to sleep, being afraid that any time she might start screaming, the sign of an upcoming attack with the consequence for myself to leave the house and fetch the doctor in the middle of the night.

With the help of an injection she received temporary relief and finally some sleep. I could not fall asleep immediately and was alone with my thoughts, resting on the old sofa in the kitchen, waiting for a miracle that could rescue me from painful thoughts and reality.

I was afraid of having to attend school the next morning, knowing I might fall asleep during class, giving false answers to my teacher's concerned questions and would not overhear the giggle of some classmates.

Altogether, I was upset about my situation plus my mother's aggression towards me even though I took care of all the chores with no verbal complained but in my mind, not realizing that our difference resulted from her mental and physical situation plus permanent headaches.

In school I was considered being "different" by the girls in my class and isolated myself into my own created little world, dreaming about the future when time would give me my freedom with the age of 21.

The illness of my mother escalated to a point, where she could not stay at home any longer, she needed an operation. During the 50th not many operations for brain tumor had been successfully performed due to lack of scientific knowledge. Her health insurance had run out of funds, and my father had to agree to experimental surgery, the payment for her operation. In 1959 my mother was the first human being who went into surgery without given anesthesia. A piece of wood was given to her to bite on before her skull was being opened with a chisel.

My Father's Determination to Survive

I was a toddler the time my father returned from Siberia where he had spent three years in Russian imprisonment, close to the Chinese border. My mother was happy and relieved after years of worries and uncertainty, not knowing if he ever would return home after being missing in action.

My father had survived with few others the harshness of the Siberian winters, the Russians cruel treatment to the German prisoners, the deprivation of any nourishing food or warm clothing.

His hatred toward his enemies was his motivation to survive, to prove that nobody under any circumstances would break the spirit of an SS soldier. He was stripped of his status but still in possession of his mind. At his arrival at the camp he had met an old man, a Russian prisoner who had been incarcerated for a couple of years due to his political beliefs and conviction.

My father already had the knowledge of the basic Russian language and was able to communicate with the old man, taking and following his advice. The lack of food drove prisoners to desperate actions, not being aware of the consequences that would result from eating grass to prevent them from starvation. Their entire body became covered with blisters and poisoned by the soiled grass that consequently led to their death.

My father learned a lot about the mentality of the Russian people and their judgment about the Germans. One episode I was told over and over by my father, making a statement about his strength, discipline and personal pride of being German. On his way to Siberia, prisoners were only able to stand in an overfilled cattle car without given food or water for days, unable to use any facilities.

One day the train stopped at a station and prisoners were permitted to step outside, the chance to relieve themselves. They witnessed a group of Russian officers receiving their rations out of a huge steaming field kitchen at the opposite platform. Not having had anything to eat for days, everybody who was still able to walk or run tried to make it as fast as they were able across the rails towards the officers, crying and falling down on their knees, begging with their outcry for food.

All they received was laughter and merciless kicks to their bodies.

My father was observing the sad scenario still standing at the cattle car, resisting temptation with his iron will and pride. He rather would have died before depriving himself of his dignity, begging his enemies for food. One of the officers spotted him, came over to my father, patted him on the shoulder and handed him his ration. At that very moment two soldiers were facing each other with understanding, and for a short moment respecting one another's personal values.

When my father returned home from Russian imprisonment, his physical condition did not reveal the former handsome soldier who proudly and with all of his conviction had shared and followed the idea of Adolf Hitler, to be part of a war that would protect and save his country from cultural destruction, to eliminate everything ugly and to improve all areas of live, creating a new epoch of healthy and beautiful people, the elite German race.

The destruction of his country and the lost war did not erase the former Nazi doctrines from my father's mind, still believing that he had fought the right war, implicating the cleaning of the Jews and demerit life. He still believed in the elimination of inferior people and tried to justify himself by reaching out to men who still shared the same conviction, who could not let go of the NS ideals that had poisoned and possessed their minds for years. These people had one thing in common, to glorify the past and pretend that there only was an armistice agreement and not a lost war, fantasizing about personal achievements and heroic actions while hiding in a smoke filled room betting on horse races, forbidden by law.

He became part of this crowd and tried to leave home frequently, his way of coping with reality. He could not bear the loss of war, the exchange from his beloved uniform into a simple suit with nothing but a handkerchief pocket at the spot that once exhibited several medals collected due to heroic achievements, topped with the Iron Cross.

The only way to find praise was in the eyes of his little daughter who absorbed his colorful heroic stories and was given the privilege to play with his shiny medals. Even though his wish for a boy had not been answered, his little girl had inherited his facial features, and in his vane and egotistical mind he raised her as a boy, determined to enforce his conviction into the little girl's mind, making her strong and tough and taught her to be better than anybody else, raised her with "Butterbrot und Peitsche" (buttered bread and whip, an old German expression).

The little girl was named his "Tin Soldier" and was eager to listen to his stories. She had been alone in her young life and mistook her father's attention for love. Many times she became reminded that she had blue blood running through her veins, being part of the superior race. The little girl did not understand the meaning, only that she was special and had to prove it to her father. Early in life she learned how to capture his attention by teasingly asking in an innocent way to be shown his Iron Cross and to be told stories about Uncle Adolf.

She knew that during those moments of euphoric enthusiasm he might forget about her having violated some of his rules that she had not to be afraid of punishment. Early in life she painfully learned how to control punishment when he was unable to control his anger that often led into uncontrollable rage. In moments like these, he locked the kitchen door from the inside, reached for the iron poker next to the old wood burning stove in the kitchen, releasing his anger by beating the little girl, pretending she was a boy.

The more she cried, the more blows to her small body she had to endure, learning early that he only would stop when she was able to control her pain without screaming and shading a tear.

Sometimes she had no idea why being punished, she just excepted that it was part of having to learn the values of being special, accepting that only obedience, loyalty, honor and strength would lead to represent such outstanding human beings.

He could not stand weakness.

As long as I remember, my father pointed out to me that my mother and sister did not have the strength the two of us shared, they were just considered being weak, in lack of education and willpower, just being females. My Mother had been such a beautiful woman before the war started but all the hardship she had faced while replacing her husband during his years of being lost in action had left some marks on her face and body.

Now she had to listen to her husband's accusation in the presence of her little girl, to be negligent about her own appearance and to let herself go. The little girl often was torn between pitying her mother who never had time for her and the lecture about strength her father already had implanted in her brain. She had no chance but taking his side, maybe because not wanting to be like her mother, or being afraid of becoming shunned by her father, his special punishment by withdrawing his attention for days, leaving the little girl with a troubled conscience. He always succeeded in his manipulating way, breaking the little girl's spirit, turning her into his puppet.

One day while playing on the street, one of the boys tried to take her ball and insulted her by swearing against her father. They got into a fight and the little girl had to take a beating, running home crying to inform her father about the insult. Instead of praising her for her defense, her father rewarded her with more beating, telling her that from now on she had to give the beating to the boys and never again to come home crying. I guess that was the beginning the little girl started to think and act as a boy, in order to please her father.

My father named his teaching lectures, hours of learning, mostly during rainy or uncomfortable days with no chance to play outside.

The little girl was taught all capital cities of the world including all continents and had to know them by heart. She also knew how to read the clock long before she entered into grammar school. But most of the time she had to listen to his heroic war stories, remembering places and cities and had to point them out on the map.

He always made sure that the Jews were connected with his stories, emphasizing their status as a cancer that is spreading all over the world, a parasite, a bacillus that would infect the entire society. Another reason for their punishment was their financial power that had enabled them to buy and take over German family businesses after the Great War, buying farms and accompanying land that had been in German families over generations, enough reasons for their elimination.

The little girl did not quite understand but believed everything she was told while being brainwashed. Sometimes the lectures became interrupted by the noise of trucks belonging to the armed forces, passing in front of our house on their way to their exercise area.

My father always got up from his chair in moments like that, walked up to the window, clinched his fists with his knuckles almost turning white and yelled through the closed window: "Fu..., bastards!" –, reminding the little girl not to forget that those were her mortal enemies.

One day, one of their trucks had to stop right in front of our house in order to change a flat tire, a reason for most of the soldiers to jump off the truck for a cigarette break. The little girl who had been playing close by, ran over to the soldiers and said with a smile on her face: "Fu..., bastards" –, not knowing about the meaning except its relation to the soldiers.

For a moment there was an absolute silence before all the men broke into a roaring laughter, filling up the little girl's apron with goods she had never seen before: chocolate, chewing gum, corned beef, white bread and packs of cigarettes. Overwhelmed with joy and full of excitement she held tight to all the goods over filling her apron, already thinking of the pleasant reaction and praise she might earn from her parents.

The moment her father saw the foreign goods, he yelled: "Don't you ever come home again with presents given by our enemies!"

The little girl was very sad and did not understand, all she wanted was some praise from her father instead of blame.

Another time when the soldiers drove by and recognized the little girl playing, they stopped their vehicle and came over to her bringing their fellow men, waiting for the reaction on their faces after having heard the little girl saying with a smile on her face: "Fu..., bastard."

This time she only would keep the chocolate for herself, hiding it from her father and give the rest of the presents to a neighbor's kid.

The little girl had to learn the same rules and proper behavior of the upper class her great grandmother once had handed over to her father. In her young age she knew about etiquette, the right behavior at the kitchen table, to sit upright without talking, only to respond while been asked, and always to use her eating utensils in the right manner.

She had no way to compare her upbringing with other children while living with her parents. In all those years she never was permitted to invite any kids to her small apartment or attending the birthday party of any neighbor child.

Still, the little girl was content in her own fantasy world, chasing after simple beauty that would make her happy. During summertime she loved to visit the meadow connected with a small farm at the outskirts of the city, not too far from her place, where countless marguerites would stretch their modest faces to the sun and invite to lay down next to them. The little girl always had to look out for the farmer who lived close by and had chased her away before.

It always was magical to her, resting amongst the tall grass with beautiful white flowers next to her. Sometimes she had to lie down, keeping her eyes closed while father sun tried to enhance the freckles on her face, and sometimes she was able to see figures and faces in the soaring clouds above her. The meadow was an escape from reality, a haven, where for a short while she would find peace and freedom from pressure, freedom among its endless beauty.

The little girl always had the need to pick some flowers, to stay connected with its beauty for a little while before nature would do its part and let them wilt away. Actually, she felt sorry for having to detach their stems from the roots in order to be with them for a short time longer. She talked to them and excused herself before she carefully would pick one after another to create a huge bunch, wrapping a blade of grass around their stems to keep them from falling apart.

Another favorite place was the cornfield nearby with the crop reaching above the little girl's head while walking slowly along its rows. She knew it was forbidden to play in the fields and with this kind of knowledge she slowly moved among its gigantic stalks while gently pushing them apart. During times when being on her own, she was just a little girl, trading the outdoors for missing toys, chasing after butterflies instead of her father's praise.

Sometimes she acted like children use to act when they are small, she picked her nose in the presence of her father. She knew it was considered not proper to pick ones nose in front of people, and at once she was asked by her father: "Why do you pick your nose, do you have a Jew inside?"

To her a foreign object (like a "bugger" they say in the States) inside of her nose had been named a Jude (Jew) by her parents, and only in her teenage years she understood the discriminating connection still being upheld by her father and mother.

Her teenage years opened her eyes and mind to all the discriminating spoken and unspoken relations to people considered as "Untermenschen" by her father, people who did not belong to the Aryan race. She remembered the gypsies who had gathered their wagon on a meadow outside the city, in walking distance for the little girl. To her it was forbidden to have any contact with "Zigeunerkinder" (children of gypsies) or to play close to their camp.

The little girl was fascinated by their colorful but ragged clothing and their long black untamed hair that framed beautiful dark faces with sparkling eyes, almost black as coals. Many times she had walked to their place against her father's will, hiding behind a tree while listening to strange songs, sung by happy people. She remembered the first time she had watched the wagon drive by her house and asked her father about those different looking people.

He took one of his war pictures out of the box hidden in the back of the bedroom's wardrobe, depicting people who wore ragged clothing, dancing on a railroad track in front of German soldiers with rifles pointing in their direction.

This picture was taken in Rumania my father said. We made them dance for us before we took them away, a bunch of worthless gypsies, "Untermenschen" who will steal anything that was not secured.

Once in a while the adult son of our landlady would throw a party. He had moved back into his mother's house and occupied the room across the small hall in front of our one bedroom apartment. Everybody considered him being a drunk, the best customer of his own moonlighting. Most of all the neighbors would show up for free liquor and dance to American big band music played by the radio. My father always called it "Nigger Music" and only participated when Glenn Miller's sentimental journey would be the background for German lyrics:

In Hamburg ist ein Negerkind geboren,
von oben bis unten schwarz kariert,
seht ihn an den kleinen Arsch mit Ohren,
wie er zittert, wie er friert.

(English Version):
A Negro child is born in Hamburg,
from top to bottom checked black and white.
Look at him, the little ass with ears,
how he is shaking, how he is freezing.

A Journey Into my Past

I was on my way to face my memories. In order to write about the most wonderful times during my youth, I had decided to visit my sister who resides in a tiny community close to my grandparents' former home.

To book my ticket in advance meant a deduction of 50 % on the regular fair plus a seat in the first class compartment, a chance to experience all the comfort and luxury I cannot afford under normal circumstances. Looking forward to find a place in the dining car where tables with white tablecloth and fresh flowers in small vases invite to relaxed dining.

The train will start slowly, leaving the small village I have chosen to find quietness while writing the happenings from my child hood. I had asked for a window seat to be able to enjoy the entire view of the southern part of the country I was born in. Our train moves with ease through mountains split by tunnels and giving view to endless rows of pine-trees, the pride of the Black Forest.

I had used this train before several times while visiting my oldest son and grandchildren. Whenever I had boarded one of Germany's famous trains, the pendant to the "Bullet Train" in Japan, I sadly remembered the excitement listening to the noise of a moaning engine that had left its mark in a little girl's mind from early train rides, when locomotives had to be fed with coals. After a while the forest makes way to wide-open meadows with small traditional farms nested within, decorated with flower boxes overfilled by bright red blooming geranium. One is always overwhelmed by the beauty of nature, in an area that appears utterly withdrawn from reality of time. It seems that our train has gained strength from this special beauty itself, now encouraging its engine to higher speed.

Two or three hours have gone by, and meadows give way to endless fields of grain and different crops, interrupted by some larger cities. We will make our first stop, time for me to change trains. Shortly after having walked through the tunnel that leads to the next platform I anticipate the arrival of the next train with butterflies in my stomach, knowing it would take me close to the area where I had traded sadness with happiness for few years in my youth, in my grandparents' village.

The second train offers the same comfortable environment and I am relaxing in my reclining seat, going back in time with my memory about the upcoming next short stop at the city famous for the art academy I had attended almost forty years ago. In the distance I can already get a glimpse of "Hercules", the tall monument situated on a small mountain top, representing the city that still inhabits many art students, eager to make a difference in society by transposing their creativity into their chosen occupation.

I always had been reflecting to the sculpture as the gentle giant who now is reminding of the time in winter when the kids and I had climbed that hill with our sled, full of anticipation to slide down without interruption. A smile enhances my face to memories gathering unforgettable moments of a young mother having been so proud to belong to one of the best art academies Germany had to offer.

A few hours later, new memories will come to mind. Our train had reached the area of Northern Germany where I was born, the surroundings I grew up in. I guess, my emotions are split, one part is excited to be home? I am not sure if I really mean it, or it's just the excitement of knowing the place and only good memories I will permit to appear in front of my inner eye: memories of Friederich, my grandfather.

How could I ever forget my very first encounter with the man who became my role model, the man with the wide-open heart on my mind. How could I forget the moment he called me "Heikelein" while lifting me up close to his face where I got tickled by his thick moustache, his very personal pride. All of his life he took good care of it, and during my staying at the farm I loved to watch him cutting and grooming his moustache by moistening the ends with his spit and twirling them between his fingers to make them stand upright.

Grandpa still was considered a handsome man in his second part of life with his white hair cut short, complementing his freckled face. It always was hard to decide whether his reddish moustache or his smiling green eyes were the focal point of his radiant appearance. Nobody will ever know how much I missed him since my youth. He was the love of my life and whenever moments of depression hindered my strength to continue, I talked to him and my mind and weary heart received peace.

My sister was the lucky one, she grew up being around the presence of my grandparents while I was waiting and anticipating the arrival of summer school vacation, the chance to be send to the farm to be close to them for few weeks. Those weeks were limited.

When I turned twelve, my grandfather passed away, and grand-mother never was the same again. She followed him a year later, close to the same day he had died. My wonderful grandparents were gone, only memories of the most carefree times in my youth had survived and gave me strength to overcome years of searching to find a place to belong, for my children and myself.

I always will have the urge to return to that special place as long as time will be given to me, to feel the presence of the two most wonder-ful people who let me forget for a little while the cruel expectations of my father.

The train had reduced its speed and would be ready to stop soon at the station of a larger city, about 20 miles north of the small village were my grandparents and their parents had found their last rest at the old cemetery. I wish it still could be the old train station that had been shut down with several other public institutions due to rationalization of infrastructure. I remember the old station connected with memorable excitement I felt as a kid when listening to the combined noise of the whistle and engine announcing their arrival at the station.

This high tech electric train would not leave visible sparks enforced by the iron wheels sliding along the tracks or release its last steamy relief before coming to a halt. Those memories of the old train station where locomotives with its simple and modest technology had given joy to children like myself and turned some of us into romantic fools.

After leaving the train I can see my sister standing next to her husband at the end of the station waving at me with both arms up in the air.

The last time we had met was several years ago and to see her again gives me goose bumps, my sign of affection and love I felt for her. We would spend a couple of weeks together with the chance to create a closer bond and maybe we could talk things out about our parents and the past. During our childhood not many opportunities were given to feel like sisters, plus her age difference made it more difficult. It felt good seeing her again and I was amazed how much she did resemble our mother.

Between my sister and myself was no visible recognition of being siblings, she resembled the looks and personality of our mother in contrast to me who had inherited the feature and extrovert personality of our father. In our youth we rarely saw each other, only a few times at Christmas time when she did not share a mutual enthusiasm about some simple presents, nor my way to play by making up games. It probably had to do with being ahead of me with five years in age.

All those thoughts went through my head while taking an unfamiliar road to their place and I promised myself to visit more frequently to make up for lost years when feelings about my sister had not the intensity. It was different now due to both of us had become of age and appeared to be more calm. On our way to their place we did not talk much except about my train ride and mutual interest about each other's well-being.

Actually, we never had talked much with each other. If I started a conversation involving our parents, I could sense her uncomfortable feelings and determination to change the subject. Sometimes it was unavoidable to mention our parents and she eagerly pointed out the hardship our mother had to endure, making sure that my father's actions toward our mother had not been forgotten in her memory.

I guess we never had shared a mutual interest about anything except our striving for perfection.

Both of us had this incredible need to excel in our daily duties and both of us had this drive to clean house when not needed, a manic behavior I have tried to get rid of since years. My sister never asked for anything besides the attention of her family by verbalizing her daily duty, making sure that everybody would recognize her engagement toward her loved ones who probably did not realize her desperate need for attention.

Her father had failed her, and by talking out loud about all her daily duties was her own confirmatory relief needed to cope with the past.

When I was young I admired her drawings and once became punished by my art teacher, pretending that I had drawn a picture created by her hand. She had no chance for developing her creativity or attending high school while growing up in the small village, the price she had to pay for not being alone or to feel the pain of an empty stomach. She always was protected and safe around my Grandparents, the environment I had yearned for from the first day I had visited the farm. Both, my brother in law and my sister went to the same school having been friends since grammar school and later sweethearts.

After my sister had finished school she was given the opportunity to become trained as a seamstress in a larger city in Southern Germany. After a few months her home sickness had overpowered her mind and degenerated into a physical illness. She left the big city and went back to her former home where she felt safe and protected.

She got married to her sweetheart and lived for several years in the village. To raise their children, please their neighbors, work hard and save money for their retirement was a satisfying life style and daily duty.

They are good parents of two adult daughters and three grandchildren. Their oldest daughter together with her family share the upper part in a large and comfortable home, a former school building located in the next small village, bought by my brother in law several years after their marriage.

For many years I had felt sorry for my sister for missing the excitement by exploring new places. Now I am certain that her long established lifestyle had fulfilled her need for security while I was still roaming around the world, feeling restless like a gipsy. It saddened me, but I did not feel sorry for myself having lived the hardship some people have to endure before they are ready to receive their gift of wisdom. If I ever should be granted such gift, I hope it will be a combination of love, understanding and generosity like the legacy my grandfather had left for me.

Many activities come to mind while driving along the country side. I think of Friederich and all of the love and fun we once shared, how he motivated my imagination and influenced my development for my future life.

Tomorrow will be Sunday and I am looking forward to fetch one of several bikes filling one corner of the three car garage in front of my sister's home and ride the four miles to my grandparents' village to be part of Sundays service at the beautiful old church that was built in 1585 entirely out of fieldstones of various sizes. I will not sit in front, where I used to sit next to "Friederich", but will chose the bench in the very back, searching for a little girl who is sitting in first row, real close to her grandfather.

My inner soul will experience again the beauty and peace of the holy environment this little girl always had admired with awe when she often felt being watched by all the saints framing both sides of the nave (like I said before, as a little girl I always was troubled by a guilty conscience, never knew why). After the service I will walk down Main Street where asphalt surface had replaced the old road paved with cobble stones, just wide enough for two horse carriages able to pass each other.

For a short while I will linger in front of house No. 6, the place that once belonged to my grandparents, now home of people who are strangers to me. The building had undergone quite a transformation from the time a green two piece wooden door attached with a huge iron door handle and a small opening in the upper part always had invited to a wonderful Sunday dinner after church. Wooden beams were exchanged by modern bricks and the chestnut tree planted by my grandpa next to the entry door in front of the house had been cut down and replaced by a car port.

Ten years ago I had visited the old cemetery were my grand-parents were buried to rest in peace. I remember how the former small village had been changed to modern standard, in my opinion a clean and sterile place missing the harmony and beauty I felt connected with the time when grandpa and I had left church on Sundays. I still can feel the bond between us during our quiet walk home with no need to talk but holding hands. Half the way home he smiled at me, knowing of my anticipation for grandma's cooking, to me the permission to let go of his hand and run home. It took my entire strength and the weight of my small body to push down the antique iron door handle before grandma could come to the rescue.

Even before reaching our house, the smell and aroma of the Sunday roast combined with special spices and fresh herbs picked out of her herb garden next to the flower bed made me run faster. I still can visualize Grandma wearing her special Sunday outfit, a dark blue white dotted dress protected by her Sunday apron that showed tasteful embroidery around the bottom and sides and starched ribbons tied into a bow behind her waist.

During the week my aunt usually did the cooking, but on Sundays the cast iron stove was grandma's domain. She always had the perfect timing by just putting her finish touch to the delicious sauce before we would sit down at the table. Without being asked, just by observing the look on my face, she let me have a taste from the wooden spoon, the magic tool that always was part of her mouthwatering creations.

Patience was hard, never a virtue I could get used to and I always asked the same question I had asked many Sundays before: "Is dinner ready? When can we eat, can I carry the plates to the 'gute Stube' and help to set the table? Or has everything already been arranged 'in der guten Stube'?" (the room we only used on Sundays).

In order to get to the "gute Stube" one had to cross the hall and climb a few wooden steps. Their planks gave away a repeated squeak that just vanished before entering the door into the room that always had left its sublime appearance in my memory. Not only because of the wonderful food we had on Sundays, but more so for games my grandpa and I used to play secretly, trying not to get caught by my aunt who always got mad when we used the room reserved for Sundays or visitors.

We had to sneak up quietly, trying hard to avoid the steps we knew could give us away. Grandpa always made it more exciting by taking me by my hand, pretending to step on a noisy plank. And before I could open my mouth to release a childish scream, he already had changed his step to make the right choice. Whenever I had entered the room, my eyes instantly got caught by the large sized painting of "The Last Supper" decorating the right wall in parallel direction to the dining table. My next view always moved into the left corner, where the black cast iron stove with filigree motives of small animals was placed below the open square, a mutual place for the coffee pot and antique iron that needed to be filled with hot coals in the bottom before it could be used to shrink the huge pile of cloth to be ironed by my aunt during the week.

I always had to use my imagination for an excuse to visit her while ironing, a chance to explore the "forbidden room". The most unforgettable memory to the "gute Stube" was the time when grandpa and I had sneaked up without telling my aunt, our secret mission for playing our favorite game. He always had let me win so I could receive the dime as my reward. We sat down, opposite from each other, apart by the enormous length of the dining table. I put my chin down on its surface with my mouth wide-open, waiting for the moment my grandpa would roll a small ball he had formed from aluminum paper and tried to shoot it straight into my mouth.

This was the best game ever. After he succeeded, it was my turn, and I wish I could explain in words the pleasure I felt, being so close to Friederich who gave me confidence by letting me win, but most of all by giving me his personal time without any expectations but the smile on his face.

I almost forgot to talk about Sunday dinner. After we set down, my grandpa gave "Thanks" and it always seemed like a long speech. I hardly could wait to start eating after having had a small taste of it already. I do remember the wordless exchange of understanding between my grandparents, enjoying and watching the pleasure I got from eating.

This was the special time in my life, I never was hungry being at my grandparents' place. The moment I had arrived on the farm during summer vacation, my grandpa fetched his long wooden pole with an iron hook being connected to the top and reached for one of the huge ham hanging below the ceiling in the hall. He had cured the ham himself shortly after some of the pigs had reached their perfect weight to become slaughtered.

Grandma had covered those huge pieces with white cotton sacks she had sewn by hand during winter time, a necessity to prevent the ham to become soiled by the swallows' dirt. For many years the swallows had made their home below the beams in the hall, connected to the width of the ceiling.

And each year they returned to us to rebuild their nest in the same spot. I always watched grandpa balancing the pole and using all of his strength for not dropping the heavy ham. He removed the small rope wrapped around the top and finished in a loop to end up in the large iron hook screwed into the ceiling beam. Then he opened the cotton pouch and let me have the first glimpse and smell of the unforgettable aroma of this beautiful ham. He had to lift it up and cradled it in his left arm, before he used his large butcher knife and cut a big piece along one of the ends.

It still makes my mouth water just thinking of these unforgettable moments when his sharp knife changed the light brown color of the outer skin into light pink with white stripes. He cut a big piece and kept it on top of his knife, encouraging me to grab it and put it right into my mouth. I still can taste it and I never had the same taste since.

Grandma also gave me some excitement, asking me to follow her into the root cellar, needing my help to hold the small lantern with glass windows, protecting the burning candle inside. The root cellar was hidden below the hall, a square and roomy place covered by a low ceiling, just high enough for an adult to stand upright. The floor of the hall was made from clay, and the entrance to the root cellar was visible by a rectangle piece of wood with an iron ring bedded in a small round opening. It took both of our strength (so grandma pretended) to pull and open it to the few steps that led to the preserved bounty of summer's harvest.

The cellar released a certain smell combined with a comfortable coolness, resulting from the clay the entire room was built of. Four walls, covered with wooden shelves holding many jars of different colors and contents placed in a very need sequence and size.

Grandma always questioned me if my preference would be liver sausage or blood sausage, or maybe both? She never waited for my answer, just taking two jars. Then she turned around to the opposite shelve and asked if I preferred plums or cherries for dessert preserved in jars of clear glass, showing their colorful contents. What glorious memories! I can still feel the wonderful pain resulting from overeating! I guess, I just stuffed myself, and nobody ever stopped me.

After dinner I helped my aunt doing the dishes and always got reminded not to damage or drop a plate while carrying them downstairs into the kitchen next to the black iron old pump with the long brass handle and spout above the square stone basin. Small rivers of pumped water over years had created a small dip along the middle leading to the drainage hole in the back rim that gave way for the water into the flower garden.

I loved the old pump with the white ceramic ladle hanging on its handle, the perfect kitchen utensil for catching the water direct from the spout for instant refreshment pumped from the well. It was not easy to pump and try to catch the water with the ladle at the same time, but after several wasteful tries I managed quite well. Sometimes I hurried outside into the garden so I would not miss the water being released from the drainage hole placed in the outer wall of the kitchen. Sitting close to the flower bed I watched the water making a big splash giving comfort to thirsty flowers on a hot summer day after it had hit the gigantic fieldstone below on the ground.

Again I am standing in front of my grandparents' former residence like I had done ten years ago, still expecting something to find, something that could remind me of beautiful bygone times. But wishful thinking cannot change the present into the past, and I had to accept the reality and preserve the picture perfect memories in my mind.

The entire house has been transformed to modern standard, now a home to people who are strangers to me. I am saddened that beautiful exposed beams have been exchanged with red bricks and I decided the entire building looks tasteless. Many questions will be without an answer, questions related to my personal view to nature and beauty. Where might the swallows have disappeared to? The old chestnut tree had been cut down and made place for a car port.

I miss the grape vine in front of the house trying to find its way around the window belonging to the "gute Stube" and I recall my impatience and readyness to taste the grapes before they had reached their sweetness. I close my eyes again and visualize myself, pushing that long broom grandpa had made himself by connecting a bunch of birch branches about 20 inches in length to a perfectly sized limb from a tree he had found in the forest. I watched him wrapping the small rope several times in a very tight and symmetrical distance around the birch branches and the finished broom looked to me like wearing a necklace.

Saturday afternoon after lunch time the street in front of the house had to be swept before each family would enjoy their coffee time. This tradition has been exercised as long as I remember and was always a good reason to volunteer and kill time until grandma called for "coffee time". At first I needed to fetch the old bucket used for this job. The cobble stones had to be sprinkled with water first, making it easier to sweep the small piles of horse and cow manure being left by the daily traffic of animals. Each day the farm people guided their cows along Main Street to the meadows which framed the wide river that run next to the little village.

During summer vacation most of the children became cowherds and I remember all the ideas we came up with to create and invent new games. The sweeping of the cobble stones started at the edge of our flower and vegetable garden connected to the right side of the farm. It was a beautiful garden with flowers on the left side next to the kitchen wall and vegetable on the opposite side interrupted by a small path grandmother had created by walking in small steps, both feet cloth to each other.

She also made a path around the herb garden planted next to the flower bed. Grandpa had protected this small acre with an iron fence. One of my favorite places was the rose hip bush inside next to the small gate, a place for me to sit and braid my crown made from flowers after I had collected a bunch of daisies which had multiplied over the years in grandma's garden. I loved to sit down below the rose hip bush with its expanding branches reaching over the fence, inviting to its small but bright red fruit which grandma used for making delicious jam. Before I started to sweep the street on Saturday afternoon I filled the bucket with water, using my right hand to sprinkle the water with the same movement I would feed chickens.

Then I started at the edge of the garden and swept in front of the house until I reached the neighbor's place where my duty ended. Now it was his turn to continue from the beginning to the end of his property where his neighbor took over. Main street ended at the dairy, the last building before one reaches another dirt road framed by fruit trees on both sides leading to a fork with the option to end up at the meadows along the river, or the next community about four miles away.

Having been so happy around this kind of environment and life style, everything was normal, perfect and beautiful to me, even the gathering of the dirt into the shuffle that was used to deliver the contents on top of the manure pile. Grandpa had decided to put its location behind the farm next to the fenced-in pig pen and hen house, meaning, I had to walk around the fenced-in garden with the big shuffle in my hands overfilled with manure to be added to the manure-pile, ending up in valuable compost for the garden.

Most of the small farms gathered on Main Street kept their manure pile in front of their house and I remember an incident when some farm boys had made fun of me because I spoke High German, a dialect sounding different from their own. Having been very tomboyish in my youth I never was afraid of the opposite sex nor a good fight.

Push came to show, and the poor boy I was engaged with in a fight had lost one of his wooden shoes. To me it was an opportunity to grab it and throw on top of the manure pile in front of the house our fight had happened. From that day on I had earned the respect of the farm boys and was accepted in their circle.

During my work I already was thinking of grandmother, knowing that she was busy in the kitchen, preparing the voluminous black cake plate with sugar, apple or plumstrudel topped with flakes of butter. She would carry the plate on top of her head walking in a very upright position across the street to the bakery. There it would be placed into the oven together with more plates belonging to individual farm women who had carried them as well on top of their head.

It took about an hour to bake, a cruel and never-ending waiting period for a little girl. The wonderful smell of dough consisting of butter, fruit and combined spices, sometimes let me linger close to the oven until the expanding heat filled the bakery and became too uncomfortable.

The old chestnut tree in front of our house was one of my secret hiding places. I always climbed up half-way to the top where a big limb had created a small platform, perfect for hiding from my aunt who always found a reason to punish me with her long willow cane after I must have done something wrong that did not suit little girls. I was used to physical punishment and strictness by my father and never complained to my grandparents about the beatings I received from my aunt or father. Around them I always was troubled by a bad conscience resulting from their rage I often had to endure. There was not enough balance in my life besides grandpa and grandma I thought and wondered if my sister had to endure the same strictness.

Before the hour had passed, I run back to the bakery, waiting for the moment the baker opened that big black cast-iron door, using the long wooden pole with a rectangle flat top to check if the plates were ready to be taken out. I ran home immediately to tell Grandma she could get it. But I knew better, it took a short while more until Grandma could pick it up.

The plate had to cool down first, another time of endless moments for a little girl. When Grandma finally handed me my plate with the most delicious slice of sugar cake cut between dents filled with melted butter and topped with almond slivers, I just thought I had the best time ever in my young life. To me my grandparents' place was wonderful, safe and full of never-ending surprises. For a short while I was cradled with love.

Sometimes, when the weather did not cooperate with my hopes to play outside, grandpa would fetch an empty tin, reach into his pocket for a piece of chewing-tobacco (that's exactly how he spoke the word tobacco) sit down in his old leather armchair and check for the mark we had cut into the clay floor in front of him the time before playing the same game. Right there on the very spot I placed the empty tin, waiting until my grandpa had stopped chewing, ready for the big moment.

Each time I held my breath, waiting if grandpa would succeed, using all of his spit he had accumulated from the chewing-tobacco by aiming for the tin. Wow! He had done it again, right into the middle and the mark on the clay floor was history, topped by a new record.

Grandfather Friederich was an artist, who carved my wooden shoes, colored them red and finished them with white daisies he painted on top, knowing those always had been my favorite flowers.

He also was the butcher for the small village, going from one farm to another taking care of the cows and pigs needed to be butchered. He was named the "Old Dod" meaning, the old dead, related to his work.

On his route he wore his butcher uniform consisting of dark blue denim with small light blue stripes covered by his leather apron. With awe I watched him carry the huge butcher knife and shiny steel around his hip, stuck in an old leather pouch that already showed its time of use. It hung kind of loose, reminding me of a cowboy wearing his holster.

While I am writing about his steel, I am looking at it, hanging next to me at the wall. The shaft is cast from engraved brass ending with a formed cow head with curved horns on top, the opening for the leather loop. Several years ago the steel was given to me by sister and I consider it to be my most precious possession I have ever owned, a companion to me where ever I will be.

The first time my grandpa took me along to a neighbor's farm I was not afraid watching him performing his job. Before we went, he had sat me on his knee, preparing me by explaining that people did raise pigs and cows for their own consumption in order to have food on the table.

Everything grandpa did was ok with me even more since he had told me where our ham came from after the pig had been killed by a fast and skilled plunge to the neck, it was hung upside down to let the blood drain into the oval shaped wooden trough.

The farmer's wife had to stir the blood instantly while grandpa split the pig wide-open into halves removing the innards. It took all day long to prepare the meat for different uses and to make sausage by filling the washed and cleaned case from the pig.

Whenever he had to do his job, he made sure to bring me a present, two little sausages especially made for me. He called them "Pingelwuerste", meaning: two small sausages strung together.

Another duty of his was to look after the forest, I guess, one can say he was a forest ranger. That was the time he put on his green hunting uniform, shouldered his rifle and took me by my hand.

He explained the variety of trees belonging to the forest by showing me their different leaves. He introduced me to the birds and animals to get to know me. He had this great gift of teaching by introducing knowledge in a combination of humor, fun and excitement, always in a playful way a child could relate to.

In his wonderful way he taught me to respect nature and treat animals like human beings.

He had so much love inside, not only for the Good Lord and people, but for the environment and life itself.

Grandfather

You fought as a soldier in the trenches of France
longing for freedom, for laughter, for dance.
Strong as a tree, almost bursting for pride,
the man with the wide-open heart on my mind.

You took my hand and helped me to see:
the flowers, the fish, the birds in the tree,
the smile of the sun that created the shadow,
the small little snake at the edge of the meadow.

You read me the stories of the "Father of Waters",
the Indians, the war, about coal miners' daughters.
I set on your knees only four years old,
imagine the places I have been told.

You opened my heart for the beauty, for love,
for people and my Heavenly Father above.

But now I am lost, oh love of my life,
please, send me your wisdom and help me to strive
after things I saw with your eyes as a kid –
I need you, my Grandfather – as I always did.

In loving memory to my Grandfather

Friederich

Friederich, my grandfather, lived with his wife and oldest daughter in a small village in the northern part of Germany where he was born. To me it always was the most exciting and happiest place to be, starting when I was four years old and for the very first time put on the bus to go for a visit. Friederich was a simple man, connected with nature and people, one of many soldiers who fought in France during World War I.

Fortunately he survived World War I and returned home to his family.

Farmers called him to their farm in order to kill their cows or pigs, and he always was known as "The old Dod", which is old German, meaning: the old dead, related to his work. When I visited my grandparents during my summer vacation, the farm people called me: "Dod's Heike".

Besides being a butcher he took the duty as the forest ranger with weekly rounds looking after trees and animals. I loved to accompany him, admiring his green uniform with shining brass buttons, his matching cap and shouldered rifle. For each job he wore a special uniform, resembling his very duty at that very time. It always was a lengthy walk for reaching the forest and sometimes we had to stop and convert with farmers along the way.

Another companion was "Tell" his hunting dog, who already had been with grandpa for many years as a dedicated friend. He always followed, leaving a small distance between us for not showing his weakness but grandpa knew when to rest for a while for Tell to regain some strength.

In a small community everybody knew each other, and they liked grandpa and respected him for being a kind, honest and thoughtful man. His repertoire of unique and artistic handcraft earned him the admiration of his fellow men which were not too much gifted to use their hands besides farming the land.

Main Street was framed to both sides by small farms with their manure pile in front next to the entry door. All houses stood close to each other only interrupted by a gutter out of stone leading and connecting the rain water coming from each roof to another gutter along Main Street.

This small space between the farms was a favorite hiding place to us kids when playing hide and seek, and a perfect place to splash around during a summer rain.

The dairy was the last house on Main Street, a great place to hang around, watching the farmers deliver their milk in huge shiny metal cans which they carried up to the ramp in front of the building. The milk was fresh from the cow and still warm, ready to be processed by people wearing rubber boots up to their knees and a long rubber apron to protect their clothing.

I used to watch them doing their job by walking around in puddles of milk, spilled from overfilling. The processed milk was poured into the cans after they had been cleaned and sterilized with hot steam. During and after the war only "Magermilch" (free of fat) was not always available in the city and too expensive to afford daily. When my parents could manage I was asked to buy half a liter at the small dairy store around the corner. On my way home I always took a big swallow, trying not to spill this beautiful tasty white stuff.

Thinking about the past and especially grandpa, I had walked up to the former dairy, now a vacant building, only the long stony ramp with two stairs along each side reminded of hard working farmers lining up along the ramp in their open wagons, delivering the daily milk, part of their income.

I left the village behind and reached the dirt road framed on both sides by fruit trees. Half a century ago to me the trees already had seemed tall and lined up like soldiers along the way. Now, it was a pleasure standing next to them after so many years, admiring their height and girth that had expanded. It seemed like some were reaching out to the next one with their branches. Maybe they are giving comfort to each other for having outlived little children who could not wait to eat their delicious fruit.

Nobody had ever claimed ownership of the trees when I was young and everybody could participate at harvest time and keep all the apples or pears one could pick. I wonder if children still would come and anticipate the taste and pick apples like we did (Or did time have an impact on the fruit and its flavor?).

The very first time I visited grandpa, the two of us had gathered many apples after a strong wind had shaken the trees and dropped the ripe ones into the ditch covered with tall grass, a challenge for us to find all of them. Grandpa and I had carried baskets he himself had woven from willow branches.

My basket was special. Grandpa had peeled off the bark of the branches in order to add a unique pattern to its simple beauty. He had crafted it just for me in proportion to my size and easy to carry.

Every time an old episode comes to mind, another memory popped up, takes over and replaces the one I had just mentioned, making myself wonder if I had left out anything.

When I had reached the point where the fork splits the road I had to decide which direction to take. I chose the one to the right leading to the meadows along the river where grazing cows still were grazing, belonging to a few people who had expanded their fathers' farms and bought up the land from small farmers. Most of them not able to make ends meet had moved away, trying to find a job in the nearest town.

The meadows still looked the same to me, only some wire had been changed to fence in larger spaces. I thought of the time when the baker's daughter from across the street and I had herded cows along the river. Her father owned the only bakery in town across the street from grandpa's farm, and her mother run the small convenient store situated in the front part of their house. Both of her parents always had been very kind to me, but I liked her mother best, maybe because of her generosity she always had shown towards me.

Her daughter Luise and I had to lead the animals along Main Street to the meadows thinking of the provision her mom had lavishly put into two small paper bags, one for my friend and one for me.

Sometimes, I already took a bite shortly after having left the stables, when temptation took over, thinking about the mouthwatering treasure besides the old horse blankets and several other items we each carried in our bags.

My girl-friend's mother knew that I preferred a certain kind of pastry displayed behind the counter wrapped in white paper napkins and placed in a basket lined with cotton cloth bordered by hand crochet lace. "Nussecken" cookies baked with walnuts bedded in chewy dough covered with chocolate and shaped like a triangle.

As an adult I tried to find them in various bakeries, but I guess it was our baker's secret recipe he never had shared or given away.

The cows knew their route toward the meadows where we would spend several hours to let them graze. They always took their time while slowly walking along the cobblestones, dropping their steamy patties along the way. My friend Luise and I both carried a willow branch to lead them to the right side of the road in case a wagon or carriage needed to pass.

Having reached the meadow we unfolded the blankets, placed one on the ground and tightened the second one to the wooden corner post, a connection for wires to either side. We gathered a few field stones around the bottom of the blanket, supporting our small little hideaway from strong winds we had encountered lots of times before.

It always was important to me to pick some wild flowers I placed into an old jar with no more use for grandma because a crack around the rim. Luise and I always found some interesting items inside the old barn connected to their house to decorate our little tent.

The hideaway was bordered by the river in short distance from the water where the meadow was covered with cow patties. It felt like walking on a sponge along the path leading to the spot where the animals had their watering hole, a small bay where shallow water exposed shiny pebble stones. We tried to find some of flat shape in hope to make them jump several times while throwing them real close above the surface.

I felt the same emotions that once had overwhelmed my innocent heart and free spirit, giving homage to the beauty and simplicity of nature that had provided endless possibilities for imaginative games to play. I wish I could still remember the conversation between my friend and myself, but I do remember the feelings while dreaming when carefree days were limited.

After I had lingered by the bay for a while I walked along the river banks leaving the water to my left, full of hope and anticipation to find the pond where grandpa and I had collected a special grass for braiding a fly-swat. The location was still at the same spot, except the water had disappeared a long time ago and with it a haven and hotbed for tadpoles and small frogs jumping happily among water lilies.

Now the entire area was covered with tall reed and only memories are left of the time when grandpa and I had walked around the pond, selecting "Binsen" of equal length gathering them in his basket.

At home we would sit next to each other on a wooden bench beside the outhouse in the back of the farm where the pig stall, hen house and manure pile gave away a particular odor I always connected with memorable moments longing for the farm when being back in the city.

The "Binsen" he used for braiding had to be moist and flexible in order to be bent for using. At first he started with the top by combining several "Binsen" to a square before weaving back and forth, intertwining the pieces like mending a hole in a sock. The ends became split into three parts for braiding the handle. It was always such an excitement watching Friederich using the offering of nature to create simplicity and beauty.

Another favorite place to spend time was the swing grandpa had tightened to the middle beam, a supporting part of the tilted roof that covered the open walkway leading to the back, passing two small doors to the left on its way. Behind the first one was grandpa's workshop, a place I only entered together with Friederich when father sun needed to rest. To me it always was special, a privilege to a little girl who was eager to learn all about the tools hanging above the joiner's bench and full of admiration and awe for certain objects he had created after her vacation had ended the year before when she had to leave for the city.

Grandpa always supported my curiosity by implicating my help in some of his projects, a stepping stone for my future interests and development.

When grandpa was not around I often enjoyed the swing made from an oak board with an uneven side turned to the back. Two strong ropes supported the swing, running through a hole drilled at each side of the board and ending in a knot below. The second door next to grandpa's workshop covered the outhouse. In order to swing, one had to open its door to achieve higher distance. We called it the "daring game" by forcing the swing to perform to its limit.

Sometimes Luise from the bakery would come over, and together we would sit on the swing, twisting around on the spot until there was no more free space left apart from both ropes. By lifting the feet of the ground, the swing in fast motion would twirl back to its normal setting leaving us almost dizzy. We did not realize the damage being done to the ropes, and one day it happened to Luise who tried to outswing the distance I had reached before, a childish competition between us. Being high up in the air, the rope to the left ripped apart and Luise found herself screaming but safe on top of the manure pile, a questionable place for a rescue.

After she had managed to slide down, both of us could not withhold a loud laughter not only because of the change of color on her cloth but also because the smell of the "steaming pile" had left as a souvenir. I guess we both had different worries after such an unusual incidence.

My thoughts were connected with the damaged swing and my explanation to grandpa about Luise's tragedy. My grandparents never ever had reacted with anger nor laid a hand on me, but having done something wrong, subconsciously in my mind I expected physical punishment equal to the beating my father always gave me after I had done something wrong or had failed his expectations.

Grandfather just smiled while listening to my colorful story about Luise's encounter with the manure pile and decided her ending on top was a good scare to both of us and enough lecture for the future. Grandpa's generosity had always amazed me and today I know that only a person with the love to God, people and nature will receive the wisdom that Friederich had been blessed with.

After having left the pond, my attention was still given to the meadow in order to avoid some cow paddies would cover my shoes. I was thinking of a certain meadow mushroom grandpa and I had collected for grandma who would prepare them into a delicious side dish combined of champignons, onions and small diced cured ham. We still were celebrating summer, several weeks away from fall when nature would provide the seasonal delicacies on various parts of the meadows.

My thoughts connected with my grandparents always implicated the food I had tasted for the first time when visiting the farm. Fresh milk, home made ham, sausage and preserved meat in jars belonged to the daily diet of the people living of the land, produce and meat only affordable to rich folks in the city.

If poor people had certain goods valuable to farmers, they had the chance to trade in exchange for food. Thinking of food, I should not forget to mention the fresh eggs provided by our happy chickens which seemed to enjoy their freedom by releasing a steady cackle during the daily adventure to find some worms around premises. No matter where they did roam, came evening they all went back into their hen house following their protective leader, a proud and aggressive rooster showing off his colorful plumage while performing short dancing steps around his hens. By lifting his left leg, he strangely expressed his status with a powerful "Kikeriki" after he successfully had guided his entourage into the hen house exact the same time every day he made sure that none of his hens were missing.

Each evening he showed his dominant position by demanding to be first in line on top of the beam next to his favorite hen at their resting place for the night. I enjoyed tremendously the time I spend with my grandparents on the farm, close to the animals, connected with the beauty of nature and the chance to let my spirit sore, care free and escape for a while the lectures and bombardment of doctrines evil people blinded by hatred had created, exercised and enforced onto others.

I had reached the dirt road that would lead me away from the meadows back into the village, close to the old church. The small path was bordered to each side with fields of potatoes and tall grown corn providing wind protection to some vegetable gardens showing off their crop. A long row of bright yellow sunflowers with brown faces had turned their head towards the sun, away from their colorful competition of smaller flowers with equal beauty, spreading their sweet aroma among the gardens, the second home to beautiful butterflies.

Along my way I could not help touching the corn in a gentle way like I had done as a child while walking and hiding inside, protected and invisible to my aunt who always would find a reason to punish me.

Almost fifty years have passed and with it memories with no reason for keeping. Others with negative impact had lingered for a long time, raping my mind with recurrent nightmares. Memories about grandpa and the farm, the small village surrounded by modest nature with its valuable lessons freely given to people with an open mind and heart that became the remedy in times when helplessness had overpowered my entire being and weakness had become my worst enemy.

The dedication of love and kindness given by my grandpa must have been carved into my mind by an invisible sculptor who out of love had blessed a little girl with never fading memories.

During the second part of the 14th century the first farmers settled in the village and out of protection built their farms next to each other. With limited space left within their community and recurrent high water from the river, gardens were laid out close to the village.

At the beginning of the 17th century the first barns were built to store the crop and to protect the seeds and agricultural implement. The buildings consisted of oak beams filled with clay and roofed with wooden tiles from former field burns. All barns were lined up so they could be reached by single ships. During the 19th century the barns became extended by removing the inner walls to gain space for higher yield.

Today the "Barn Quarter" still existing of 28 buildings preserved and protected by the government is a favorable place for visitors. To us children the barns offered endless possibilities for play and fun among its complex grounds. People still can have fun while gathering for a Bar-B-Q in front of these buildings who give tribute to a gone by era, the time when hard working farmers gathered in the grass for their lunch break, leaning against the buildings to find shade from the sun. And maybe they could prelong their precious time for a couple of minutes to reward themselves with a good pipe (as Friederich used to say).

On my way home to my sister I would stop at the barn quarter and sit for a while on a bench next to the Bar-B-Q pit built to invite visitors, thinking about the time when I watched the arrival of the wagons filled to the top with sugar beets. During war time sugar beets became the basic for the production of sugar beet syrup, a spread (like marmalade) still an essential product available in grocery stores.

I will remember the time when I sat next to grandpa on the small bench in front of the wagon filled with hay, an additional source of feed for the cows during winter. The hay would be stored in the hay-loft located above the ceiling of each farm. One had to drive the wagon inside the hall and place it below the hatch, the opening to the hayloft.

It was very common that neighbors helped each other. The farmers were dressed in their bibs or overalls carrying their wooden rake like a rifle over their right shoulder, walking ahead of the women who were dressed in long skirts and long aprons. The entire crowd wore straw heads pulled deep down their forehead still giving view to faces that showed the impact of the sun's power.

After long hours of raking hay to be filled in the wagons, the crowd walked home and I remember the women carrying the empty water bottles and bread tins that had kept their provisions. Grandpa always let me share one of his sandwiches grandma had wrapped in parchment paper together with a dill pickle and placed in his bread box that was dented from the use of many years.

When the sun went down and evening had ended another day in the country, most of the farmers lingered around discussing their yield and how fortunate they had been that rain had not interrupted their day.

I feel like I am still able to smell the aroma of grandpa's pipe he enjoyed smoking after a hard day's work, while grandma was busy preparing supper in the kitchen.

Grandpa let me stay with him, and it always was interesting to watch the behavior of some men who could not wait to unscrew the flask that had been hidden in one of their overall pockets. One would take a long swallow of the good home brewed weed schnapps before he shared the bottle with their fellow man standing next to him.

All my thoughts are connected with my grandpa, the man who sheltered me with his love and was able to relate to my thoughts and inner feelings. The more I think about him, the more memories come to mind while sitting in front of the barn quarter.

I remember the time when grandpa thought it was a good time for the fish to bite. The two of us walked to the riverbank with our pockets full of bread. We went to the small bay were we could sit down and throw small pieces of bread into the water, broken off a stale loaf grandma had handed us with a smile, knowing what would happen after a couple of days.

We went to the same place for about a week, throwing small pieces of bread into the water, luring the fish to reappear for an easy daily meal. The day finally came when grandpa took his fishing net, (a long stick with a net tightened to a wire rim) plus a filled water bucket that we both shared carrying to the small bay where the fish already seemed to be waiting.

We sat down at the same spot and grandpa encouraged me to keep quiet for a while, a hard task for a little girl's mind occupied by anticipating all the exciting happenings. It was so easy to fill up the bucket. All grandpa had to do was putting the fishing pole into the water and catch one fish after another to give a big thrill to his little granddaughter.

I guess grandma already was thinking about all the fish and what to do with it. At first she pretended to be surprised and congratulated both of us to our big catch.

It was grandpa's duty to clean the fish, pointing out the difference about innards while I was watching him, being already excited about our evening meal.

Grandma would use one of her cast iron skillets to place above the largest opening of four cooking holes on top of the old wood-burning stove. She had to remove all three rings which gave a possibility to use different sizes of skillets or pots to be exposed direct to the fire. She would coat several pieces of fish with a mixture of egg yolk and bread crumbs and fry them in hot bacon grease until the outside had turned crisp and reached a light brown color.

At the same time she would prepare a smaller skillet with "Bratkartoffeln", a combination of leftover potatoes from the day before, cut into small slices and fried with diced bacon and onions. In addition she would decorate a plate with pickles cut lengthwise into four pieces and placed in the middle of the table next to the bread basket and milk decanter.

I still can taste grandma's wonderful creations and remember her as a quiet person who had everything under control while operating quietly in the background, in her own modest way, like my mother used to.

My memories about grandma always were connected with food. It might sound strange, but the time grandpa spent with me and grandma's wonderful cooking became one, inseparable like the two of them.

To me it was like a huge present wrapped in love. As a little girl I could sense the harmony between them, as an adult I know about the deep love they felt for each other.

I was able to spend a few Christmases at my grandparents and help baking Christmas cookies grandma stored in a rectangle tin can lined with parchment paper and stored under her bed. On cold winter evenings grandpa made sure the old wood-burning stove did its duty, a warm and comfortable place for grandma to sit close, operating the spinning wheel with her right foot while twirling the wool into a fine thread and later being winded into a huge ball, ready to be used for knitting socks or sweaters. Grandpa's reclining leather chair also had been moved closer to the fire where he sat quietly smoking his pipe, smiling and observing grandma operating her spinning wheel.

On evenings like these I thought about the cookies hidden below grandma's bed and could not help asking if nobody could steal them? I guess that was the sign for grandma to answer my hidden desire. She went into her bedroom and came back with a handful of star and moon shaped cookies she split between grandpa and me.

It was on an evening like this the first time I saw the book that had influenced my entire life from that day on. The book was huge, bound in brown leather and filled with colored pictures, depicting an American Indian on its cover. Grandpa helped me to sit on his right knee, supporting the book with his left, making it easy for me to look at the pictures while he was reading with his deep wonderful voice the stories about America, the country I would consider to be my home, 30 years later.

I learned about the Indians and their lifestyle, their connection to nature, animals and the way they lived of the land. For the first time I could see a picture of a buffalo herd roaming among the prairie and learned while braves and their families would follow them, to provide for their daily livelihood, only hunting the amount needed to feed the tribe.

Grandpa also explained to me that the Indians would not only need the meat for their survival, but use the skin to cover their tepees and to sew their clothing and moccasins and that they actually would use all the parts an animal could provide.

It was hard for me to understand why the army would fight the Indians to steel their land. To me the "Red Men" were honorable people who gave homage to nature and each living thing with the same intensity like my grandfather.

My affinity for the Native American people had intensified my imagination about the far away country, especially the southern part where one of the big rivers, the Mississippi, also called "Old Man River", was. I learned about the "Civil War" when many brave soldiers from the northern and southern part of the United States had lost their lives for the cost of freedom, to rid the nation from slavery.

As a little girl I thought of freedom as being freed of punishment, a feeling I only experienced at my grandparents. At my parents' place I was pressured by my father to be perfect, obedient and to outshine other children, to be the best. Failure often meant physical punishment, deprivation of freedom of mind and being me.

Grandfather Friederich died the same way he always had lived his life –, peaceful and in dignity. The Good Lord had blessed him by letting grandpa pass over while resting in his beloved leather chair. Three days earlier he had walked from farm to farm to visit his friends and neighbors in order to say good bye, knowing that he had to leave this world and his loved ones.

The love of my life was gone and left me with a broken heart. I was twelve years old and more troubled than ever. All of my life I had been alone, an outsider, and school had not brought the relief I had hoped for. Grandfather had gone and left me by myself.

My parents and I had taken the bus to travel in order to be part of grandpa's Funeral. We got off at the same bus stop grandpa had welcomed me, the first time ever I had visited the farm. This time it was a different season, snow had covered the ground and ditches, where pretty wildflowers had bloomed years ago during summer time, when the two of us took the long winding dirt road that led us to the farm, walking hand in hand. The picture of grandfather standing at the bus stop had always appeared in my mind when thinking of him. He was wearing his green hunting uniform with his longtime companion "Tell", his dog, by his side.

He smiled at me and said "Deern," (meaning: little girl in the old German language) "put your hand into my right pocket."

Full of surprise and anticipation I had reached into the right pocket of his uniform jacket and touched a round shiny object that appeared to be the most beautiful red apple I had ever seen.

From that moment on I sensed his deep warmth and love my grandfather always had shared with me as long as I had the privilege of being close to him.

This time there was no smiling grandfather to welcome me, this time I had come to say goodbye, empty-handed and saddened by grief and deprived by winter, unable to pick the wildflowers I had loved and gathered together with grandpa on my way to meet my grand-mother. I could not help my tears while walking the snow covered road that ended at the river.

My comfort was my memory, thinking of the moment grandpa and I had reached the river, looking for grandpa's friend who operated the ferry that just had touched the opposite river banks. With two fingers between his lips, grandpa whistled at his friend who acknowledged our presence with his arm in the air. For the first time in my life I had seen an old fashioned ferry with its small rescue boat connected at the right side, both made from wood.

It took a little while until the ferry had come back to pick up some new passengers, this time only the two of us. Grandpa Friederich introduced me as "Dod's Heike" to Wilhelm the Ferry man, his long-time friend, since both had attended the same classroom in their youth. I was amazed by the Ferry man's face, exposed to seasons of sun, rain and snow which had changed his skin into smooth leather, carved with deep ruins, especially around the edge of his eyes, telling that he was a happy man.

This time Uncle Wilhelm (I had called him since our first encounter) offered his condolences to my parents and turned to me. Without saying a word, he laid his callused hand on top of my head and stood with me for a while, knowing how much I would miss my beloved grandfather.

The Ferry had crossed the river and reached its landing point where the dirt road continued, leading to the small village. From the distance I already could see the top of the former fortress, where year after year storks had built their nests to raise their young.

Decades ago, a small section of the fortress (or castle) had been used to school the children of the village. Three generations after another my family had attended the same classroom and their picture had been taken at the same spot the day they became enrolled in school.

After a while we had reached the village and it had stopped snowing. The dirt road now was covered with cobblestones and con-sidered Main Street. It started at the old church and ended at the dairy, about one mile apart. My grandparents' farm was located in the middle at the right side of the street, and the closer we got the more I could feel my heart beat. I did not know what to expect, not even could image.

My mother knocked at the door and someone let us inside. The entire hallway was filled with loudly talking people and tobacco smoke. I recognized mostly men, neighbors, and among them the pastor of the small church. Everybody was dressed in black and appeared being stiff and uncomfortable having changed from overalls into their black suit they only would wear on Sundays and sad occasions like this one.

I looked for my grandmother and found her in the kitchen among all the farm wives who placed their home cooked food at the table. Grandma had changed, her upright stature had sunk together and she had run out of tears. I was not the only one who had lost the love of my life, we both had to cope with reality that grandpa, her beloved Friederich, was gone. Grandma took me into her arms and asked if I would like to see grandpa to say goodbye?

One of the rooms had been emptied for the Wake and appeared to me cool and real dark. Grandpa was laid out in an open, simple wooden casket, with his hands crossed above his chest, holding some flowers. He was dressed in his suit he wore to church on Sundays, and the room was decorated with white lilies.

I had never seen a dead person before, and there was my grandfather, pale and motionless like being asleep, and that very moment I realized he would never wake up again. His moustache was twirled upside at the ends like he always had taken care of it himself, and I thought of times when I had fun, twirling it myself while being a little girl sitting on grandpa's knee.

I thought of his laughter when I pleased him with a small shy kiss placed on his red moustache. Within moments all wonderful memories appeared like a movie in front of me, and I knew I still would talk to him and ask for his help in troubled times.

Grandma had entered the room and told me that I had to go now, but I still wasn't able to find the right words for saying goodbye forever. The only thing I knew that would please him was my last shy kiss on his moustache.

The funeral procession was lead by four horses in front of the open black carriage decorated with flowers, giving view to grandpa's closed casket. I remember walking next to my grandmother, mother and sister behind the carriage, and I was amazed about all the people who had followed on this cold day along Main Street towards the cemetery to give their last respect to a kind and modest man whose life focus was to please the Lord and love his family and neighbors.

My tears came back, the moment his casket left the ground and vanished below, and I knew, life would not be the same.

The next time I went to the farm with my parents was at my grandmother's funeral. She had passed one year later, almost to the day my grandfather had died. My grandmother had given up. Unable to overcome the loss of her husband, plus being dependent on her oldest daughter had taken her will to continue living.

I had never been fond of my aunt, not only because that she always had found a reason to give me a good beating, but the way she had treated my grandparents.

As long as grandpa was still alive, she had to control herself, but since he had passed on, she showed no respect to her mother, treating her with an abusive language, disrespect and neglecting her needs. From that time on, my sister was alone with my aunt, depending on her for a few more years until she got married to her childhood sweetheart.

When I Was a Teenager

I remember the following summer when my classmates awaited the upcoming school holidays with excitement and contemplation of taken vacations with their parents, while I was overcome with utter sadness. All those former years I had counted the days when six weeks never seemed to be enough. This time I actually was afraid of having to spend six long weeks all by myself, left with memories of wonderful years at the farm, and the longing for my grandfather.

Two years ago my father had to make the decision if I should attend high school or continue my education at elementary school with the only chance in future life for a low paid job or the possibility of finding a husband.

In those days only children of rich parents, who could afford the annual fees, had the privilege to attend high school after having successfully absolved the required intelligence test. My parents had lived of welfare for many years, unable to pay money for my education, even though my father was determined to show off his daughter who always had been an excellent student in elementary school.

Trying to help my father's eager wish to see me in high school, I found a job at the local tennis court, collecting tennis balls every afternoon after school, my contribution to the required high school fees. I liked my job at the tennis court where people treated me nicely and paid my service and effort with good tips. During breaks between games, I was permitted to use an old racket for practice at the wall and learned the game.

I remember several years ago, I must have been in second grade in elementary school, my father had found a low paid job, shuffling coals to heat a boiler in an English General's basement. He called it a disgrace, and for several years to come my mother and myself had to pay for it, being remembered over and over of him having accepted a low paid job as a laborer from an employer he once had called his deadly enemy.

His job lasted about for a year due to an accident. My father had emptied the bed of a truck filled with coals. The moment he wanted to jump off, the driver had started to move the vehicle, not recognizing my father was stuck on the truck. He ended up with a slipped disc and was hospitalized over several months. After his release he was handicapped, obstructed by an iron corset, unable to work for years to come.

I remember the day I came home with my certificate, proud and excited to please my father that I was one of the smart children who had successfully passed the entry exam to high school, one of forty percent. High school was quite a challenge in many ways.

This time I was part of thirty girls raised in upper class families, dressed in nice clothing. Some girls who believed to be better than others, had formed a clique, a circle of privileged class mates selected by appearance.

In elementary school they liked me, especially the boys who had admired my toughness while playing soccer in difference to the girls in class. Then I did not care if someone made fun of my clothing handed down from my older sister, my strength was in my mind and my fists, giving me my own satisfaction in situations if needed.

My elementary teacher was a wonderful man I was very fond of and I went out of my way to please him with excellent grades. It was so easy to like him opposite to my father, and sometimes I had wished he was my father. To me he showed the same kindness I knew from my grandfather, and like him he had called me with a nickname related to my eyes. He called me "Rehlein", meaning: little fawn.

Another reason for liking elementary school was the lunch handed out to children from families with low income. The qualifying children had to carry their "Henkelmann" to school, an oval shaped white ceramic container with its lid fastened by a clip on each side. We used to carry it connected to our knapsack or satchel, and I remember the certain noise during walking when it hit the clasp below the right side where the shoulder belt was connected.

There were mostly boys and only three girls living in our neighborhood, and we all attended the same elementary school in different classrooms. The girls always used to walk together, ignoring me, so I walked with the boys and shared their games on the streets after school. This time it was different, there were no boys in my classroom, and the three girls who also had passed the entry exam, still ignored me.

The high school was situated in mid-town, next to a beautiful old church where I received my confirmation when I was 13 years old.

The first day in school we each had to stand up, saying our names and tell the occupation of our fathers. I remember the giggling of the girls and the surprised eyebrow rising look behind the glasses of my teacher after he stated the occupation of my father: laborer. This was the beginning of discriminating and cruel situations during my future school years.

Having reached my teen hood and being around girls who already had eyes for the opposite sex, I got kind of confused by the obvious difference in our appearance. Most of them were dressed in the last fashion, while I still wore clothing my older sister had outgrown. I pretended not to care, but my pride had been questioned, and the longing to belong and not being different already lingered in my mind and was hard to overcome while being locked out of the crowd.

There was nobody to confide in except the daughter of our landlady who was childless and sometimes took care of me after coming home from school. She knew that both of my parents were absent during the day, my mother cleaning house at an upper class family, and my father always late. After his iron corset had been released, he went back to his favorite vice, gambling at the horses. Many times after school she had asked me inside her place she shared with her mother, our landlady, and fed me lunch.

Their apartment was comfortable and had made an impact on me, especially the paintings at the wall. My eyes always got focused on one picture, depicting an Angel with spread arms, guiding two small children on a bridge, crossing a river. I still can visualize the painting in front of my eyes and feel the same blessing, believing in Angels.

The other picture at the next wall showed a bowl overfilled with different kind of fruit, and the shining red apples always reminded me of my grandfather. I did miss him so much, and my wonderful memories spent comfort to my troubled soul.

Aunt Lieschen, I called our landlady's daughter, sometimes had slipped a "Groschen" (equal to a dime) into my hand which I exchanged for a piece of pastry at the bakery next door.

My birthday was in the middle of June, and each year on that special day I could not wait to get home, running the entire way in anticipation of the bowl of fresh strawberries picked from their garden –, my birthday present.

On that special day the table always was decorated with flowers on top of a white table cloth and set with shiny crystal and a silver spoon for my personal use. There always was a second bowl on the table, filled with fresh whipped cream, and the moment I started to taste the strawberries I did not mind missing a real birthday celebration with children, this was alright with me.

In my entire childhood I was not permitted to invite any children to my home, nor attend a birthday party of other children. Once I had an invitation to be present at the birthday of a girl whose father owned the only paint shop not too far from our home and knew my father.

Against his will and without a present I went anyway with the result receiving a severe beating after coming home. Having always been told to be special and proud of it, I still was unable comprehending the limitations of such privilege forced into my mind.

Years later I understood the reason of my upbringing in difference to other children. Both, my mother and I never had a chance of being socially involved with other people.

As long as I remember we were distant from reality due to my father's stupid pride. He still was too involved with Germany's history to admit he ended up a looser after such a heroic past. He never permitted having any visitors who might have wondered about our meager living situation and questioned his vanity. Having been lonely from my childhood on I had related to my own imagination inside my own little world.

But I had become a teenager, almost reached adulthood and part of a different environment but same intellect I was used to former teachings by my father.

Even though I was not selected being part of the "Clique", I had made some impression to some teachers who had been sensitive to my feelings of not belonging but eager to fit in. The only way for me was to show my equality by being smart and liked.

My favorite subjects became English studies, sports (physical education), German studies plus history. German history changed my view about my upbringing with false pride, SS doctrines and cruel determination by my father to create his little "Tin Soldier". Subconsciously I started to rebel against him, escalating into utter contempt.

My favorite teacher became a young lady who taught English and sports. We were educated with Oxford English. In order to pronounce it the proper way, we pretended to have a hot potato inside our throat. Trying to impress her, I started to write poetry, using simple words from my limited vocabulary to express my feelings, becoming the teacher's pet.

Finally, I gained the respect I thought, turning out to be just jealousy.

Still reaching out for acceptance I turned into a "Sad Clown", trying to cope with my isolation by entertaining others and myself. To me it was easy to joke about things, situations and myself, realizing the cynical joke of my entire life.

From Tin Soldier to Teenager

My entire life I wanted to fit in, secured by my feelings to be invisible like everybody else, part of the crowd. No matter what I had tried to overcome my being different from other children, everything had failed. The influential teachings of my father had backfired, to be tough, strong, intelligent and better than others and had created a visible young person, sticking out and being rejected by the crowd, in this case her classmates, with the exception of one girl.

She was sitting in front of me during class, a girl not being part of the special clique, rather kind and friendly. Sometimes she took me home after school before I had to leave for the tennis cord to pick up balls for the players.

For the first time I understood the function of a family, a real family. Her father came home each day for lunch, acknowledging his loved ones with a kiss and inviting myself with a smile to be part at their table to share the food. Lunch always had been considered the main meal of the day until our civilization had been changed by prosperity and fast food. To be invited into the home of my classmate always meant something special, remembered and carried with me during my adulthood, a kindness resembling the comfort at my grandparents' home.

Twice a year our entire class took a fieldtrip to one of the sights not too far within our environment. There was a small mountain range in walking distance of a few miles depicting the monument of a famous German Emperor on top of its crest, visible for miles away and a place for cultural interest. It was a long walk among meadows and fields of various crop bordered by red poppies and blue corn flowers.

The trip was planned by our class teacher, the one who educated us in German studies, history and religion. Next to our enjoyment of being released from class for one day, our experience later had to be remembered on paper. Once, while standing on top of the steps to the monument, looking across the scenery, the fields and meadows appeared to be colorful carpets which I also mentioned in my essay. From that day on my class teacher sometimes asked me to read lyrics by his favorite German poets in front of the class. To be noticed by my German and English teachers as well as my class mate's family made me proud and happy.

We always were encouraged to bring a lunch package for our field trip. Some of the girls always showed off and exchanged their "delicatessen", boiled eggs, fruit, cold fried pork shops and a bottle of coke, quite a difference to my modest sandwich.

After Monika and her parents had shown their kindness, I called her my friend and accompanied her during our trip to the mountain. Before we had reached our half-way resting point, she secretly handed me a lunch package her mother had especially prepared for me, consisting of cold meat, boiled eggs and fruit, an exceptional memory to a gift of consideration, kindness and honesty.

During my years in high school I always looked forward to educational sports taught by my English teacher who had studied abroad and was familiar with games still unknown to German children.

We all loved to learn and to play baseball and basketball and did not mind having to carry the heavy basketball poles with the net connected sideways at the top, to the open arena next to our schoolyard, the place where annually the big circus puts up its tents and animal cages.

Sometimes I try to remember things about my French and Geography teachers, two elderly women, unmarried and with an attitude of a spinster. I was not liked very much by them, and my feelings were mutual due to their remarks about my clothing and my looks, undermining my effort to please them with excellent grades. As a result I was receiving grades my father was not to be pleased with, enough reason to receive his punishment.

With time the special clique adjusted their attitude towards me, trying to be part of my team while playing basketball and asked for my help with their homework in exchange for some change of their allowance. My parents could not afford monthly pocket money, and sometimes I kept a special tip I had received at the tennis cord in order to buy sweets.

There was one specific situation in high school at the time I anticipated my confirmation at the Evangelical church situated next to school. My family has been of Lutheran faith, which only my grandparents had publicly celebrated. My mother had prayed with me, vaguely in my memory while being a toddler, but grandpa and grandma let me still think of the same words they had prayed with me, the same once prayed with their daughter, my mother:

Ich bin klein, mein Herz mach rein,
soll niemand drin wohnen als Jesus allein.
Amen

(English Version)
I am small, please cleanse my heart,
Nobody shall live inside, but Jesus.
Amen

A few days before my Confirmation the attitude of my class mates had changed. Somehow I sensed a connection to my person by their mimic and words unspoken, but reflected in their eyes. Something ought to happen, but I was clueless, with ambivalent feelings. The situation seemed to increase the moment our English lesson started and my teacher had entered the classroom, carrying a large package.

After we all had answered her "Good Morning, girls," with our "Good Morning" to her, I was asked to come in front of the classroom.

My first thought was: what did I do wrong? A question I always had asked myself in uncomfortable situations when my father's rage became intensified and when he paid special attention to me. This time I felt no guilt but awkward while walking from my bench in the back towards the front, passing giggling girls sitting next to the isle.

The load on my shoulder became released with my English teacher's smile. She asked me to her desk where she had placed the package when entering the classroom. It was an impressive looking package, wrapped in expensive paper held together by a red ribbon, knotted in a bow, and I wondered what I was to do. When she asked me to open it, butterflies started to appear inside my stomach, and I felt being excited and helpless the same time.

Carefully I started to release the knot, trying hard not to damage the paper, while realizing the change of excitement within the class-room. It was a silence like having to write a dictation during German studies, and I wondered why. To some girls my unwrapping seemed to be too slow, encouraging me to hurry and rip off the paper.

It was such pretty paper and I ended up folding it back by using the same creases. Before I could look at the contents, my teacher told me that this was a present she had selected, a present for my Confirmation, bought from money she and all the girls from my entire class had collected. I opened the box and looked at a beautifully checked pleated skirt with matching sweater and cardigan.

For a moment I was speechless, only my tears could express my inner feelings and emotions. Here I was, standing helpless and exposed in front of the class, expected to say the right words, words which would be received and understood different by different individuals. This present was given to me because of my status, never ever having had anything like it before, and I still could not find the right words. This was a present of Love given by my teacher and most of the girls to see me happy in my beautiful outfit I was to wear after my Confirmation.

At the same time it was impossible to ignore the giggling and action going on between some girls who exchanged words behind their hands I did not have to imagine, I knew.

Happiness and shame filled my entire body, and that very moment I felt being naked and exposed about my entire being, my background and my parents, being poor. I never knew how to find the right words, but on one hand I felt being discriminated, and on the other hand I was grateful, happy and excited to look beautiful in an outfit I would not even have dared to dream about.

All I could say was: thank you, while trying to imagine the reaction of my parents to this present given to me. My mother was pleased, realizing her worries had been answered when I showed her my beautiful outfit. I knew she wanted me to fit in with the other girls, knowing about her inability to buy any clothing for such a special event. The reaction of my father was quite different, shouting about his present situation by referring to a better time when "Adolf" still was in power, and himself of a different status, never ever having to take any charity from anybody.

All of a sudden I remembered the situation of being a little girl playing on the street, when foreign soldiers had filled my apron with goods, and I was being admonished by my father never again to accept anything people would give to me. This time I begged, hoped and prayed he would let me keep my new outfit, and with tears in my eyes I realized the fight within himself when he gave in to my plea.

At that very moment I acknowledged my happiness would always depend on my father's moods and Vanity, and my obedience to him began to weaken.

After my Confirmation nothing really had changed in high school. Discrepancy and rivalry had not been erased by the late happening, and my state of mind became challenged by my mother's personal problems. She always had been complaining about headaches, but lately the pain had increased severely to a point, where mother had to stop working, and I felt sorry for myself.

Thinking back, high school was a privilege only for rich children and that was reality. Every day battle about discrimination, rejection and trying to fit in, required enormous strength, understanding and sensitivity in order to cope with reality, consequently a burden that only hurts. I felt miserably and believed that life had been unfair to me since birth, a shortcoming in happiness.

My Mother's Illness

While growing up, my mother seldom had a chance to pay attention to her little girl due to the conditions at home. The years of waiting for her husband to come home after being missed in action, plus the pressure having to cope with him being a changed person after his return had taken its toll on her health.

There was no gentleness left inside the man she had loved who was reliving the heroic moments of his beloved lost war, increasing his attitude into uncontrollable rage while feeling sorry for himself. Situations like those often lead to mental and physical abuse, not only laying hand on his little girl, but his wife as well. Sometimes I wonder of her illness originated of the beatings to her head.

My mother had to stop working and stayed at home. Her headaches had increased, causing her unbearable pain without escape. The doctor related her suffering to menopause, unable to detect the time bomb slowly developing in her head, prescribing pain killers.

Her husband more than ever avoided to be home, his wife's illness had awaken his attitude towards weakness, there was no compassion, only self-pity.

To me it was hard to cope with my mother's illness, she could not stand to be around people, always telling me to go outside and play when I had to do my homework. The tennis court became my second home, admiring rich people with beautiful cars and dressed in expensive cloth while I had to cater to their needs, picking up tennis balls.

My personal environment consisted of obvious contrast, high school, where discrimination belonged to my daily lessons, the tennis court where beautiful rich people with a friendly attitude towards me paid money for my service, and the everyday coming home to a meager kitchen where no one had a chance of privacy.

In addition to cruel and uncomfortable reality the wonderful memories of by gone times with my grandfather initiated my rebellious feelings against my situation, especially my father whom I blamed for all my pain and shortcoming in life.

It was the time a small fast food restaurant had opened its business close to the location to our school in midtown, serving "Pommes Frites" (French Fries) wrapped in a paper bag shaped like an ice cream cone and topped with ketchup and mayonnaise. But the most intriguing thing was the juke box in the far back corner, releasing songs like "Buena Sera" by Louis Prima, "Diana" by Paul Anka, "Lipstick on your collar" by Connie Francis, "Loving you" by Elvis, plus various hits from Rock stars like Buddy Holly, Dean Martin, The Everly Brothers, Little Richard, Ricky Nelson etc.

The music box became our hangout after school, lingering around with a portion of French fries in our hands, excited by a new and arousing rhythm released from a small disc. We all tried hard to figure out the sometimes strange lyrics and pretended to understand by singing along with refrains not quite understood compared to the English taught at school.

Rock'n Roll was capturing the imagination and feelings of all of us, and the first fast food introduced from Holland to our country became the equivalence to the American Hamburger. We all began to act like groupies during the anticipation of a new selected song activated by a single "Groschen" (dime) being slipped into the juke box, releasing a new and so far unknown rhythm that would entice our bodies to strange movements.

It was the beginning of a different era, Germany's youth had welcome Rock'n Roll with open arms from America, the country that not too long ago was one of the worst enemies of their fathers. Local DJs supported the new fad that soon would expand into a huge money making boom for the record business.

A.F.N. American Forces Network located in Frankfurt, Germany, transmitted the American Top Twenties each weekend over the radio, and teens were eager to listen and find out more about their idols. We all had picked one, but opposite to my classmates who adored Elvis, I had fallen for Ricky Nelson who had released "Mary Lou" and "Poor Little Fool", my all-time favorite songs.

My father could notice the difference in my behavior when I tried to sing, releasing his frustration by shouting about the influence of American Nigger Music had transformed German Youth into monkeys.

At that particular time my parents did not own a radio, and without ever telling I went on weekends to one of my former soccer bodies' home, listening to American Top Twenties. During those moments I was released for a while from my regimental upbringing, soaking up tunes which seemed to soothe my tensions, giving way to my first acknowledgement to the opposite sex.

Wulf

The first time I noticed his smile into my direction was at the right side of the juke box where boys from the local gymnasium of classical language had gathered, flirting towards our group of class-mates in their own shy way. His appearance resembled the incarna-tion of the perfect Aryan, the type of men I would notice amongst people for the rest of my life.

I guess, the influential lesson and teachings by my father about Hitler's perfect race had painted a picture I saw in front of me, close to the juke box, and I was overwhelmed by the tension that went right into my stomach.

All of a sudden I was worried about my looks, questioning my cloth and shoes formerly belonging to my sister. I knew that I had grown up becoming a tall, good looking teenager, but that very moment my confidence collapsed and I thought I would die when he started to walk into my direction.

His name was Wulf, tall, blond with blue eyes and two years older than me, a strait student at the gymnasium, determined to become a physician. We both found out being almost neighbors, living in the same area, only a few streets apart. He asked me if he could walk me home, but I was glad that my afternoon was occupied by working at the tennis court, a chance for not having to point out our small apart-ment and being able to avoid questions about my parents.

We saw each other frequently by chance, both pretending not hav-ing planed our next meeting at the juke box. Wulf and I became friends in an innocent way, bottling up our feelings inside and avoid-ing talks about relationships. I don't remember dating like dates would be set up between two teens.

He knew my schedule when I was home or at the tennis court and showed up randomly, increasing my heartbeat from such unintentional tease. He never rung our doorbell, he just showed up, whistling a special tune from a certain movie called "La Strada" (still considered a classic, one of the best releases by Federico Fellini). This was his way of asking me to come down and meet him.

With time we opened up to each other, talking about our situations and individual dreams for the future. Both our mothers were stricken by an illness, consequently the development of a closer bond between the two of us.

We both lived at the edge of town near an area where storks had build their nest close to the swamp, Wulf would pick me up with his bike, his camera on his shoulder, asking me to take a seat on his bike's carrier, telling me that we would interview the storks, a funny way of talking about his extra income with the finished photos ending up in the newspaper who paid his effort with a check of five German marks. Various times Wulf would show up with his Latin schoolbooks, for me to test his vocabulary. It was an innocent friendship with a developing need to be close to each other.

My father encouraged my relationship with this Teutonic looking young man from an upper class parental home situated in an expensive neighborhood. During my upbringing, teachers as well as my pastor considered prenuptial sexual relations unethical and shameful, a sin. I was committed to save myself for marriage, a reminder that always appeared when unknown desire emerged from kissing my boyfriend.

One day our doorbell rung and my father walked down the stairs to answer the door. A woman unknown to him asked the question if he had a daughter, which my father replied to her, if she had a son?

Wulf's mother had found out the location of our home to demand the ending of my relationship with her son, pointing out that he was too special for wasting his time with a low class girl who only would interfere with her higher plans for his future. She turned around and left, before my father was able to find the right words. He never mentioned his emotional reactions to her showing up at our doorstep, only pointing out to me that he contradicted her demands.

It was the time my mother's illness had evolved and it let to her first epileptical attacks that from now on happened almost daily. It always started with a scream leading to spastically attacks with no control over body and mind. Sometimes she would hurt herself on certain furniture while falling down, and sometimes she would bite her tongue, unable to talk when changing back into a normal human being.

The small kitchen became my personal room at night with the old sofa to sleep on. I did not mind, for several hours I was alone with my privacy, secured by the door that separated the kitchen from my parents, who spent their nights each in a twin bed moved together, due to the lack of space in their small bedroom.

Each night I was scared of mother's scream, the announcement of an oncoming attack, knowing I had to get up in the middle of the night, calling for the doctor who lived about twenty minutes away from our home. I knew he would take me back with him in his car, my only relief. My mother's attack came frequently and unpredicted, mostly at night. Some were short, her chance to fall asleep again without having to call for the physician.

Right now I feel sad and guilty for not having shown the compassion she deserved as my mother. I felt sorry for her but unable to show the same emotional feelings coming from my heart compared to the thoughts of my grandfather.

My father's mood swings sometimes unleashed his uncontrollable rage, insulting and blaming my mother for her illness, insinuating the clean health records of his ancestors.

High school became a burden when my class teacher noticed myself being not concentrated and falling asleep during class, and I was too ashamed to open up and talk about my mother's illness and situation at home. Since my mother had quit working, money became a bigger issue than usually, and my father had decided to take me out of school, to go to work because of our need for money.

Leaving high school appeared to be a relief in the beginning, a separation from discrimination and tease. Later on I understood that my only chance to be accepted at any university had passed.

My classroom teacher tried to convince my father to keep me in school, or at least have me tested for my skills in order to find a job connected with my abilities. The test took many hours of writing, math, painting and analyzing certain pictures with the first impression that came to mind. In addition I had to work with wooden component parts and was asked different questions by different persons. Everything combined determined my IQ and the direction to a job I would be qualified for, in my case a building planer.

I was offered job training at an architectural office with a salary next to nothing, still a great chance for a future carrier. My father denied myself this opportunity, it was just not enough money being paid right away. He still was pleased with the outcome of the exam a personal victory soothing his vanity, confirming his influence combined with former teachings that had formed his daughter.

The record store was located at the corner of a busy street in mid-town, next to a street car station. Every day people would pass their waiting time in front of the display window, gazing at posters depicted with foreign artists from England or America, selling their recent hits in tall letters.

A middle-aged, childless couple had owned the place for years selling next to their inventory of radios and early TVs, records of national artists, classical music and hits of the great American band leaders like Glenn Miller and Benny Goodman. Since they had adapted the last craze and added Rock 'n Roll music to their repertoire, their store became another hangout for Teens after school waiting to occupy one of three available headphones in order to listen to their new idols last hit, exchanging their pocket money for a small disc of music that would enhance their fantasy about a foreign country known as Milk and Honey.

So far, only one person had worked behind the record bar, the owner's wife. With improved business she was looking for another sales person and left a notice at our grocery store. Somehow my father found out about the demand and contacted the owner who decided to employ me after we became introduced to each other.

Now I was placed behind the record bar and became the latest hit for high school boys.

My father either did not care that what he called "Nigger Music" was part of my daily environment, or was convinced that such ridiculous tunes could not prevail against our German classical music and still beloved German marches, he believed the craze would vanish soon.

My work at the store had changed my attitude about waking up in the morning. I really looked forward to my job behind the record bar, acknowledging the admiration of boys from high school who had changed their hangout at the music box to visits at the store.

My boss was pleased with her choice of employee and often invited me to be part of her coffee brake which mostly took place at the small café next door where mouthwatering cakes were tempting costumers. She was a kind lady, and her regret of not having children had let her to adapt me in her own special way, helping me to forget the former discriminations experienced in high school.

She introduced me especially to classical music unfamiliar to me, since there was no receiver at our home. It took a while to connect with tunes that transmitted calmness contrary to the wild untamed rhythm of Rock 'n Roll. There was one specific record released by Earl Bostic who had turned the "Love Dream" by Franz List into a swinging, happy melody, reason to connect my interest to the real version that became one of my favorite classical tune, enticing me to classical music.

To sell discs recorded in English language, enhanced my vocabulary and the desire to find out everything about America, the country that generously had provided its former enemies with car packages full of goods I had tasted myself long time ago. And now this new German generation became introduced to a music that had loosened our regimental attitude and enticed our need for an unknown adrenaline rush.

Rock 'n Roll had doped our minds and bodies and became the drug for all of us non-users. We were crazy for American artists who in our minds represented the country that was number one in the world. Rock 'n Roll became our outlet for missing needs. We were hungry for foreign music combined with new fashion and we started to wear bobby socks and petticoats, imitating American teens.

The Barn

While teens were experiencing Rock 'n Roll plus adapting certain behavior connected with the new era, implicated by foreign music plus foreign fashion, German business people took advantage by trying to cater to the needs and desire of German teens, who hungered for the chance to dress, dance and act like their American teenagers seen on TV.

A smart farmer had converted his empty barn into a dance hall, located in a small village, reachable by bus. The news had spread like wild fire, and soon the place was packed with young people who sat tight next to each other on simple wooden benches along wooden tables framing the huge square dance floor, sipping coke and acting cool.

If one had arrived early, one could still find an empty spot around the juke box, again, still the main attraction to everybody. The juke box was not to compare with all the beautiful painted sound machines I could admire in the States many years later, its shape was kind of square without any fancy decorations or flashing light bulbs, just simple, but loud enough to overpower any conversation. The entire building was equipped with red and yellow small light bulbs, connected to strings across the room and tightened to each corner post, creating a cosy, almost seductive ambiance.

One part of the barn was elevated to a stage where German rockers belonging to amateur bands tried to convince the spectators with a poor imitation of Elvis's songs by shaking their hips while being dressed in black leather. Others had adapted Bill Haley's look, trying to outdo Elvis's sideburns with the famous curl of his hair doe.

The "Scheune" (the Barn) had attracted many of my young customers from the record store, spending their weekends in the company of friends or school mates. It was a must to sip a coke in order to be part of the crowd, to become accepted, to belong.

Where ever young people came together, cliques were formed, and Rock 'n Roll clubs emerged like mushrooms out of the soil.

Each Saturday night a couple of each club signed up to take part at the Rock 'n Roll tournament, in hope to be crowned as king and queen.

My boyfriend Wulf always had been in company of guys from upper class families, members of the renowned local rowing club. Those boys had no means attending the Barn, their enjoyment and outlet became the vacant homes or villas of individual parents who had left town for business or short vacations.

The first time Wulf took me to attend one of those parties I was overwhelmed by such opulence, referring to their impressive lifestyle. Some of Wulf's friends I had met before as customers at the record store. I instantly became accepted and welcomed within a group of teens from a total different upbringing, in a total different environment.

For the first time I was grateful about my father's insisting teaching about etiquette and distinguished behavior, a regular routine to those kids daily circle.

We set in comfortable leather chairs and lavishly upholstered couches, some of us using the matching pillows, crowding the thick carpet close to the stereo, sipping coke, mixed with expensive cognac from ones father's liquor cabinet.

Everyone had contributed their records, but most of the time we danced to slow music equipped with sentimental lyrics, holding tight to each other, consequently getting lost in kissing.

Moments like those sometimes led to daring touching, when petting became the harmless climax to one's evolving feelings.

As long as Wulf would pick me up, my father kept quiet about my staying out late, rather encouraged me to get close to him.

Some of the girls who attended the party also were members of the rowing club, used to similar lifestyles and befriended with one of the boys. We always showed up as couples, avoiding rivalry among friends.

I experienced the best time of my teenage years, my first love, being accepted by an upper class crowd, but most of all by being left alone by my father.

At night my happiness still was clouded by worries, afraid my mother could start one of her epileptic attacks and I would have to fetch the doctor.

In such situations the memory of my last meeting with Wulf would ease my pain like when thinking of Friederich, my grandfather. I did not replace grandfather with Wulf, there was enough place for both of them inside my heart.

The time arrived when Wulf had finished gymnasium, prepared to attend one of Germany's best universities to study medicine. For months I had tried to avoid thoughts about our separation that would take the person away from me who had been my first love, best friend and confident in need, my source of happiness. His promise to stay in contact by writing, did not ease my devastated feelings, rather questioned by if I had the patience to wait daily for his mail. My loss already resulted into physical pain, a feeling I remembered so well from my grandfather's passing.

In good weather I went back to the tennis court on weekends, collecting balls and some pocket money to buy new cloth and to start saving for a bus ticket to visit Wulf sometime.

I still got invited by the upper class clique and went to their parties on rainy weekends, getting lost in sentimental songs and memories.

Since Wulf had left for the university, my father started to pay more interest about my privacy, questioning how I spend my free time.

My mother's condition had worsened to the point that one could suspect daily attacks which usually appeared in the evenings or at night. To fetch the doctor was still tiresome but not as hard as during high school.

My job at the store started at 10am, and the sound of my favorite records helped to regain lost energy. Our landlady looked after my mother during the day if needed.

Wulf's letters arrived frequently as promised and offered an insight about his daily routine at campus. He loved his studies and joined an elite student association engaged in fencing, the representative sport of the university since generations. Members of the fencing fraternity became acknowledged by wearing proudly a certain ribbon pinned to their chest, or a gash on their face, the permanent reminder of carefree play between studies. The ribbon acknowledging the student's fraternity was a promise for going study when presented to their girlfriends. Several months after Wulf had left I received his ribbon by mail in addition to his invitation to visit.

In order to reach the town of his university I required a bus ride of several hours through the country side, a pleasure to my eyes and soul. But I was on my way to visit my best friend, unable to recognize the God given beauty passing in slow motion. To me the bus ride seemed to last forever while I was occupied with lasting memories and questions about our meeting. It would be the first to stay for one night as a guest in a small hotel at the market place, close to the bus stop and university.

I still was surprised about my father's permission to stay over-night, plus admonishing me not to be stupid. Why stupid? Being ignorant would have been the right word in my position, on my way to become introduced to the big city and prospect of spending one night in a real bed.

One never is able to control upcoming thoughts, and thinking of a real bed implicated the daring wish to be with Wulf.

With his leave I was deprived of his tender kisses while our arms wrapped tightly around each other, aroused by the small bulge behind his pants.

On the other hand I was afraid of my feelings and convinced myself that his need to be close to each other was the same like mine, to be loved, to be understood. Still, I wondered if his new experiences at the university had influenced his feelings and changed his vision about the girl who deeply loved him but did not belong to his choice of intellectuals. I guess I was confused by my thoughts and hoped that Wulf would be the same as I always had known him as a convinced catholic whose conviction led him to respect mine to save myself until marriage.

Could my yearning bottled up since his leave would be reason enough to weaken my personal conviction and give in if asked?

Wulf picked me up at the bus stop, and the smile on his face wiped away all unanswered questions. He was happy to see me, carrying his heart on his shoulder while trying hard to be cool, acting like an adult by picking up my cheap small suitcase I had bought from my last money earned at the tennis court.

A small distance to my accommodation and being lost in my happiness did not give time or effort to look around the new surroundings all different from our small town. The facade of the small hotel was decorated with blooming red flowers in wooden boxes, complimentary to the exposed beams, transmitting the vision and idea of a charming and cosy hideaway.

My heartbeat started to pound the moment we arrived at the front desk and felt almost naked being exposed by the omniscient eyes of the clerk due to years of experience. The reservation was made in my name but paid by Wulf who received the key and helped me to walk upstairs the carpet covered steps, looking for my room.

Sunshine had found its way through soft curtains, enhancing the color of pretty flowers in a tasteful vase, placed on a small table next to the white linen covered pillow and comforter on top of the single bed. Wulf must have noticed my blushing and took me into his arms, comforting both of us while realizing the first opportunity of total privacy the two of us had dreamed and hoped for.

He watched me from the only chair standing in one corner of the room unpacking my few belongings which I orderly placed in the open shelf above the cloth rag, hiding my extra pair of underwear beneath my sweater. I still felt uncomfortable about my appearance in cloth outgrown by my sister and hoped that my physical looks would balance the first impression.

Incidentally Wulf asked if I liked the bouquet and the small vase, his way of telling me about his welcome present. He knew how much I loved flowers, remembering the time when we had shared the quiet and beauty of a meadow, surrounded by daisies among tall grass.

The last item out of my suitcase was my toothbrush which I held helplessly in my hand not knowing where to put it. Wulf got up and opened a small door I had not noticed during all my excitement, giving way to a tiny bathroom, furnished with a sink, toilet and shower. To be able to use a real shower before hiding beneath a feather bed was too overwhelming and almost too much. My eyes wondered around and admired the beautiful white towels with the hotel's logo embroidered in one corner while still holding my toothbrush.

Wulf took it with a smile and placed it inside the drinking glass on top of the console above the sink telling me that we had to hurry to buy some soap before closing time. I was embarrassed for not having thought about the need of soap, hoping it would be the only mistake during my visit.

Not that I was lacking self-confidence, but being in a hotel for the first time and unfamiliar with its interior and bathroom equipment, I was thinking already of how to operate the shower without asking Wulf.

To shop for soap was a perfect reason to leave the room with its silent temptation already taking over our minds. Wulf bought some soap, oval shaped and wrapped in silk paper, resembling the smell of lavender. The clerk put it in a small open paper bag attached with two handles, still giving away its aroma while being carried by me during the evening.

Finally, I was able to pay attention to certain sightseeing Wulf had chosen to point out within our short visit. We walked to the campus of the university he attended, trafficked by students between dorms. Wulf pointed out the location to his room and talked about his fraternity brothers. To observe such an environment with busy students carrying themselves in a certain way that transmitted an important status made me realize again that I would be deprived of such privilege forever.

I was born into a poor family and was unable to imagine a change of status for myself. Still I had my dreams and was grateful for the time spent with my grandfather. His love to me meant more than any money could buy. We spent the afternoon walking along small streets with beautiful shops, window shopping while holding hands. Sometimes we would stop when the opportunity was given to kiss, hiding inside an entry way, concealed to the eyes of by passers.

My emotions combined of feeling secure, understood and being loved by the person I admired and adored had overpowered the strength of my conviction, I was ready to give in to the desire of getting lost, to welcome a weakness that might lead to my fulfillment if Wulf would ask.

In my heart I was ready for the special moment when the demand of the body would be the prize for the loss of innocence, to experience the special moment when two lovers melt to one. I was ready to prove my immense love by giving my only personal possession, my virginity.

When dawn had shortened the day and intensified my imagination due to the hours being left before night, Wulf took me to a small restaurant, leading the way to a small corner table, moving one chair and helped me to sit down first, before ordering the menu for both of us. He knew me so well and helped avoiding to feel insecure about things I had never known before.

After dinner he introduced me to some of his fraternity brothers who occupied a larger round table inside another restaurant known as a student hangout. I must have passed the questioning eyes and first impression after being introduced and asked to share their round already influenced by the consumption of beer and medical terminology. Often I had helped Wulf with his Latin vocabulary studies, able to acknowledge a few terms, helping to find back to myself and overcome the intensity of an intellectual crowd.

Since I was only 16 years of age, unable to consume alcohol in public due to law, I had to sip my coke and got high on the entire situation, being with Wulf among his friends of a different status from the ones I already had met before in our home town, again, I felt being special.

We spent the entire evening among his fraternity bodies while I was thinking about the opportunity of the small bed with the clean white covered sheets and bed spread, resembling the color of innocence. The later it got, the more I became occupied by my thoughts, wondering if Wulf had the same feelings and ideas about the hours left of my visit. I guess he tried to avoid the smile and confronting unspoken questions from his friends about leaving, consequentially we stayed to the end.

We walked back to the hotel kissing and our arms holding tight around each other, providing each other with physical as well as mental support for the moments to come.

The entrance door of the hotel was closed and we had to ring for the night clerk. With few minutes left together and the realization of an opportunity lost to spend the night. Wulf's last embrace transmitted his unspoken desire I had waited for in desperation all day long. He wanted to be with me as much as I, but instead we were facing an awkward situation where the chance to sneak in together had passed.

We stood kind of helpless, not knowing what to say but "good night" when the clerk arrived with the key. Wulf left with the words "I'll be there in the morning to pick you up for breakfast".

I was numb, unable to think strait while walking up the stairs to my room. It was the kind of situation when one had anticipated and planned something extraordinary in hope to gain fulfillment. It was the kind of situation when such dream had burst like a balloon with its shreds turned into doubting questions of personal failure.

Did we purposely spend all evening with his fraternity brothers to avoid the night? But I could feel and was certain of our mutual desire only to be interrupted by fate, leaving us with our former convictions about innocence and marriage, leaving us without occurring guilt, a small relief, just enough to find sleep that night.

The next morning I woke up early and enjoyed the luxury of the bathroom. For the first time in my life I took a shower instead of a bath in the old sink tub on weekends, using the lavender soap Wulf had bought for me, accompanied by its lingering scent until it faded when I returned home.

After I had collected my few belongings I waited in the only chair for Wulf to arrive, memorizing the wonderful day we had spent, looking forward to the hours before the bus would transfer me back into reality, away from a wonderful dream.

From the distance I could hear him whistling the tunes from "La Strada", and I rushed to the window facing the street. My heart started to beat a faster rhythm connected with the sound I had waited for daily since our first encounter.

Wulf came to my room and took me into his arms, asking about my well-being, subconsciously referring to the situation late evening. I told him to be fine while hiding my blushing face on his shoulder, trying hard to avoid upcoming tears due to our unavoidable separation. We left the room, a place that could have changed our lives and personal connection, a place important enough to be remembered for the rest of my life. Wulf took my small suitcase for the last time while I carried the empty vase placed in the paper bag next to the soap, too valuable to leave after one use.

The silk paper was convenient for wrapping the bunch of flowers I carried with me to memorize hours of happiness from a visit enhanced by unspoken desire and willingness to overturn personal principle and convictions denied by fade.

We spent breakfast with rather shy conversation, trying to avoid the subject from last evening until Wulf opened up, stating that my all time former conviction about virginity and marriage was respected by him due to circumstantial happenings, except he did not feel like a hero.

Thinking back, both of us never dared to speak the three little words every person is waiting for, the promise interpreted forever lasting love and dedication.

Sometimes I had wished to be confronted by his verbal feelings, still I accepted the way it was, feeling certain of his love.

Before the bus left with its door locked, I could watch Wulf from my window seat whistling the tune from "La Strada", his personal way of announcing his arrival or departure. His tune always would linger long after he had said good bye, leaving me with a bitter sweet hurt so well known by lovers.

This time the hurt did not fade like Wulf's whistling of "La Strada" when the bus drove away from him, leaving me with his image marked forever in my heart and mind. That very day I did not know that destiny would need eleven years for our next encounter.

At home I was confronted by my father about my being with Wulf, and if we had spent the night together. I pretended with an outraged denial and finally I understood the meaning of his words when I had left. Only this time: "Don't be stupid" had changed into "I told you, you are stupid to miss the chance that could have made you the wife of a former doctor by becoming pregnant."

To comprehend the reverse reaction from my expectation to his morals was confusing and almost impossible. Deep inside I felt guilty about my willingness to give myself to Wulf only interrupted by circumstance.

Still, those facts were unknown to my father, and his reaction should have been full of praise to his daughter who had returned a virgin physically.

My father's manipulated encouragement to visit Wulf had back-fired into rage and annoyance toward his teenage daughter.

My job at the record store became influenced by love songs of certain lyrics, resembling my feelings to my daily memories of Wulf.

More than ever I yearned to be with him, overjoyed by an arriving letter but full of disappointment if days went by without receiving a small envelope transmitting his thoughts.

The reaction to my father's statement led to more disrespect I already felt, acting carelessly to certain rules I had to obey, my rebellion to his demands. One of them was the visit to the "Scheune" (barn), the Hop, were Rock 'n Roll competitions took place on weekends, awaited by teens with tolerant parents and understanding to their wishes. The others without permission still had to wait for American Top Twenties transmitted by AFN on Sundays. At the record store we were up to date with all new hits released, frequently shipped by European companies, carrying the foreign label.

My neighborly friend had exchanged our sometimes mutual excitement for Sunday afternoons listening with anticipation about our favorite musician having reached the charts. He had joined one of the Elvis Fan Clubs who idealized the "King", trying hard to continue his former mannerism by wearing a similar hair style and cloth, especially adopting his famous pelvis rotations before he had to join his country's army, stationed in Germany.

Elvis' fame had spread and outdone celebrities covering front pages. His posters placed next to James Dean, his record sales outdone all foreign artists before him.

There were some Elvis songs I liked, none of them could change my admiration for Ricky Nelson whose "There never be anyone else but you for me" played at my first dance with Wulf at his friend's party, where our feelings deepened by the soft sound combined with lyrics enhancing our unspoken feelings.

In later years I played this special song whenever moments of sadness appeared, in hope of finding calmness by its bitter sweet memories.

The name of the Barn became exchanged to "Dancing at the Hop," often asked as a question by gatherings of friends or to me during my daily work at the record store. Spending time at the tennis court had always been a good excuse, but lately customers could not understand my denial to their approach, and I felt it was my duty to show up, representing the record store. We often had tried to dance Rock 'n Roll at the parties and I always had the right feeling for music, especially when certain rhythm empowered one's body, consequently erasing one's mind, leaving the illusion of feeling free as a bird.

The first time I accompanied my childhood friend to the "Hop" I did not get caught by my father.

One had two choices to make it to the Hop, by bus or by bike, since none of the teens I knew owned a car. During my last year in school, one day my father showed up with a bike for my use to fetch the doctor at night if needed. The bike was painted in three colors, blue, white and red, colors of the Tricolor, the French national flag, consequently leading to a nick name I hated: "Franzose" (the French).

To become connected to "the French" had a negative, rather derogatory meaning in public, a reason to be used by some of my former classmates to intimidate me. After that certain incident I'd rather walk to school, even though it took about forty-five minutes.

Working at the store was different, no one noticed my bike after I arrived in the morning and left it during the day inside the storage room across the street. The Hop was an exciting place, a chance for teens to loosen up by expressing their emotions throughout individual movements on the dance floor, in balance to the rhythm.

Off the floor, the boys would hang around in groups with their hands hiding inside the pocket of their tight pants, a needed help to overcome insecure feelings in order to act cool. Most of the girls would arrive and leave together with their boyfriends but formed their own groups across the dance floor, opposite to the boys, showing off their appearance by wearing the latest fashion copied from American teenagers, giggling and debating about the coolest guy while waiting to be asked to dance.

Altogether it was a harmless environment observed by watchful eyes of the owner and his helpers. The small little village had never seen anything like it, and to change a barn into a dance hall was frivolous in farmers' minds, consequently leading to a development of outrage and false rumors.

Several times I had used the bus to be part of the crowd except for one Saturday, when teens would arrive from everywhere to participate and hopefully succeed at the biggest Rock 'n Roll tournament so far. I was worried about its timing, probably outlasting the last possible bus, my chance to get home. That day I used my bike, full of anticipation to be present the entire evening, I did not care if I got caught, I was asked by the guy with the reputation of being the best "Hotter" (dancer) to be his partner at the tournament. Well, I got caught!

My father must have found out somehow, showed up late in the evening and spotted me among the dancers. In front of everybody he beat the hell out of me. No one ever could have imagined my shame and despair when everybody stopped dancing to witness an outraged father dragging his daughter off the dance floor while the music box kept on playing "Rock around the clock".

Thinking back, the proper tune at that very moment should have been "Jailhouse Rock" as a warning to the upcoming most tragically three years of my life. I really don't remember how I got home, hurt and bruised all over; I had to follow my father on my bike, trying not to listen to his insults and threat to put me away into a reformatory. The only place where girls like me would be brought back to the former German values of brotherhood and order, now stained by the influential "Nigger Music" and superficial lifestyle of "fu… Americans".

What did I care –, any chance to be away from home must be a relief to my physical and mental pain, an opportunity to be around "girls like me", punished by similar fathers unable to detach themselves from former Nazi doctrines.

Girls like me could not be so bad I thought; all I always wanted was to be part of something, to belong. Since I remembered I was shunned by my father if not fulfilling his demands, shunned by neighbor kids for being a Nazi's daughter, and shunned by classmates for wearing second-hand cloth. Why could I not have some fun? Dancing Rock 'n Roll with all the others was only a crime in the eyes of a fanatic who still lived and defended the values of the Third Reich.

The following week went by without any indication of unusual happenings. I went to work as always wearing long sleeve shirts and pants to cover up my bruises, still afraid to face certain customers who became witness to my father's rage at the dance floor. He himself gave me his silent treatment which I preferred to endless debates over proper behavior regarding my obligation to my aristocratic inheritance. A long time ago I had realized that those facts preached by my father was only meant for himself, a chance to fall back into his elitist and dominating role as a soldier, punishing imperfection.

Aunt Lieschen was the only one I could entrust myself with all of my problems like I had for years. She was a kind and understanding person, spending comfort and motherly understanding I could not expect from my mother who always took sides with my father in fear of becoming punished herself.

Today and for many years during my past I feel so sorry about my mother for not having understood her personal turmoil. Being always rejected as a result to her illness had interfered and silenced my need for love, consequently leaving me empty and dead inside.

Becoming a mother myself has taught me that a mother's love is always present, no matter what. My mother's illness and father's interference had hindered to express her.

I am so sorry, Mom.

VS-Villingen, 20.Oktober 2009

Anhang zum Aufnahmeantrag

Sehr geehrte Frau Dieterich,

Im Jahre 1959 wurde ich von der Fürsorge in Minden /Westfalen., meinem Geburtsort, in das Erziehungsheim :
Waldheimat, Werther bei Bielefeld eingewiesen.
Meine Identität wurde gegen eine Nummer ausgetauscht, Nr. 830.
Insgesamt habe ich dort 3 Jahre verbracht ohne jegliche Kommunikation mit anderen Insassen, keine privaten Gegenstände, ein Zimmer mit Gittern vorm Fenster und ohne innere Türklinke. Kein Ausgang oder Besuche, zensierte Briefe, keine Schule, nur Arbeit täglich für 8 Stunden ohne jegliche Bezahlung. Kein Bleistift, Papier oder Buch zum Lesen, außer der Bibel.
Tägliches Frühstück: zwei Scheiben Brot, eine mit Margarine und eine Scheibe Schwarzbrot mit Zuckerrübensaft.
Das Mittagsessen war deftig, kein Fleisch oder Gemüse, nur Kohlehydrate, kein Obst.
Man bekam 20 Pfennig Fleißkärtchen die Woche die niemals reichten um Seife, Zahnpasta oder einen Apfel zu kaufen. Man wurde bestraft durch Entzug von Fleißkärtchen falls man während der Arbeit eine Schere fallen ließ, oder Kontakt zu anderen versuchte, sich aufbegehrte oder während der Arbeit seine Notdurft verrichten musste. Man durfte nur 3 x täglich zur Toilette gehen, mit jeweils nur einem Stück Zeitungspapier.
Wir haben es benutzt um uns gegenseitig Notizen zu schreiben, indem wir eine Nadel in den Finger stießen und mit unserem Blut und dem Nadelöhr geschrieben haben.
Ich habe Fingerhandschuhe für die Bundeswehr genäht, 36 Stück am Tag. Falls ich mein Pensum nicht erreichte, wurde ich bestraft.
Auch habe ich Strümpfe stricken müssen für die Bundeswehr, Männerhemden bügeln mit gestärkter Brust, bestimmtes Pensum pro Tag. Außerdem habe ich Deckchen gehäkelt und gestrickt zum Verkauf im Basar.
Mein Zimmer hatte Gittern vorm Fenster, keine innere Türlinge, einen Stuhl, ein Bett und eine Konsole mit einer Waschschüssel, gefüllt mit kaltem Wasser. Wecken, 6 Uhr früh, Zimmer putzen, waschen, antreten zum Ausgießen der Waschschüssel und des Nachttopfes.

Man wurde hart bestraft wenn man während der Nacht den Topf für Stuhlgang benutzt hatte. Danach gemeinsame Morgenandacht mit anderen Gruppen, gehalten von der Hausmutter in einer kleinen so genannten Kapelle.
Man wurde aufgerufen um Bibelverse aufzusagen die man abends vorher im Zimmer lernen musste.
Die schlimmste Bestrafung war der Karzer, genannt Butze, ein winziger Verschlag auf dem Boden, ohne Bettzeug, totale Isolation von der Gruppe über Tage, meistens nach einem Versuch wegzulaufen
Die Anstaltskleidung bestand aus grauem Kleid, Schürze und Pantoffeln.
Unsere Monatsbinden mussten wir selber stricken aus dicker Baumwolle und unsere Nummer einnähen. Man bekam 8 Stück pro Monat, die dann anschließend gewaschen wurden in der Waschküche um sie dann zurück zu bekommen. Ich habe sie immer wieder während meines Aufenthaltes benutzen müssen.
Es gab weder Schulunterricht, Ausbildung oder ärztliche Untersuchungen. Einmal, zu Beginn meines Aufenthaltes musste ich zum Arzt zur Untersuchung ob ich noch Jungfrau war.
Ständig wurde uns eingeschärft das wir Mädchen mit Vergangenheit seien, zum eigenen Schutz und zum Schutze der Gesellschaft solange erzogen werden bis wir wieder in die Gesellschaft integriert werden können.

Dies war ein kleiner Auszug aus meinem täglichen Leben während meines Aufenthaltes in der Waldheimat.
Fast hätte ich vergessen, dass eine große Mauer um den gesamten Komplex lief, und wenn wir draußen waren, Holzschuhe tragen mussten.

Außerhalb des Heimes wurden wir eingesetzt zum Kartoffelkäfer plus später Kartoffeln zu sammeln, Beeren zu suchen im Wald mit Verbot sie zu essen, und Brennnessel zu pflücken für Salate.

In meiner Kindheit wurde ich mit Nazi Doktrinen erzogen die später im heim fortgesetzt wurden. Ich habe mein eigenes Konzentrationslager durchlebt.

Mit freundlichen Grüßen,

Heike Freiwald, geb. Reher

P.S.
Ich habe mich heute mit dem ehemaligen Heim in Verbindung gesetzt um Einsicht in meine Akte zu erhalten .Mir wurde gesagt, das Akten älter als 30 Jahre zerstört seien, aber man könne mir an Hand eines bestehenden Buches meinen Heimaufenthalt mit Monat - und Jahresangabe bestätigen, in den nächsten Tagen per E-mail.
heikefreiwald@hotmail.com

Hausordnung

Den Anordnungen der Hausmutter und der Helferinnen ist pünktlich und ohne Widerrede zu gehorchen.

Die Pfleglinge dürfen niemals über ihre früheren Sünden miteinander reden.

Besondere Freundschaften einzelner werden nicht geduldet.

Kein Pflegling darf Geld, Briefmarken oder Schmucksachen ohne Erlaubnis der Hausmutter im Besitz haben. Was davon mitgebracht ist, wird beim Eintritt abgenommen und von der Hausmutter verwahrt.

Ohne Erlaubnis angenommene Geschenke werden zu Gunsten des Hauses konfisziert.

Die Hausmutter hat das Recht, alle ankommenden Briefe zu erbrechen.

Die Vermittlung einer Dienststelle ist allein Sache des Hauses. Wer mit Ehren aus dem Hause entlassen wird, wird alsdann auskömmlich mit Kleidung ausgestattet.

Tagesordnung

Im Sommer um 5 Uhr (im Winter um 6 Uhr) Aufstehen.

Diejenigen, die kein Amt haben, stricken und lernen will im Lärzimmer, die Übrigen versehen ihre Ämter.

Eine halbe Stunde nach dem Aufstehen: Kaffeetrinken und Morgenandacht.

7 – 9	Uhr:	Arbeit in Waschküche, Nähstube, Garten und Stall
9 – 9½	"	Frühstückspause
9½ – 12	"	Gemeinsame Arbeit
12 – 1	"	Mittagessen
1 – 3	"	Gemeinsame Arbeit
3 – 3½	"	Kaffeepause
3½ – 7	"	Gemeinsame Arbeit
7	"	Abendbrot

Nach dem Abendbrot verbleiben alle, die nicht anderweitig zu tun haben im Wohnzimmer, wo sie sich unter Aufsicht mit der Instandsetzung ihrer eigenen Sachen, leichten Handarbeiten und nützlicher Lektüre beschäftigen.

Unmittelbar vor dem Schlafengehen ist Abendandacht. Nach der Andacht geht jeder Pflegling still in seine Kammer und legt sich zu Bett. Eine Viertelstunde später hat alles ruhig zu sein.

(Bildquellen: Archiv/Heike Freiwald)

Application for membership at Organization of Former Institutionalized Children Germany

In 1959 I was taken to the reformatory: Waldheimat, Werther / Bielefeld initiated by the social welfare office in my hometown.
My identity became changed into Nr. 830.
I have spent three years without communication to other inmates, no personal possessions, a room with bars in front of my window and missing door handle inside my room.
There was no permission for visitations or to leave the institution.
Once a month we were given a pencil in order to write a letter to our parents. Only positive statements about the reformatory became sent after being censored by Mother superior.
There was no educational teaching, just daily controlled work of 8 to 10 hours without pay.
We weren't allowed any private things, not even paper and pencil, no books, except the bible.
Our daily breakfast consisted of two pieces of bread, one with margarine and the second to be spread with sugar beet syrup.
Even lunch did not consist of nourishments, mostly filling ingredients like flower and potatoes, very little vegetables and hardly any fruit.
By the end of the week we could have earned 20 cents if there had not been any deductions due to punishment, like dropping a pair of scissors or trying to talk to someone, to rebel or the need to use the toilette during work time.
Three times a day we were able to use the toilette, after breakfast, lunch and dinner. Newspaper was provided instead of tissue.
The white border from the paper was used by us in order to write little notes to each other by using a small needle to extract some blood from our fingertip, in order to write with the eye of the needle a small message.

During my time at the Reformatory I was given different tasks, like knitting socks and sewing gloves being used by the German Bundeswehr (German military) always under close observation of 2 sisters.

I also was placed behind an iron board to perform my daily quota of perfect starched men shirts ironed to perfection without a single crease.

Later on I was chosen to more filigree work, to knit huge tablecloth by using very thin yarn, and also create beautiful crochet work to be sold at the annual bazaar.

My tiny room had a barred window, no inside door handle, a chair, an iron bed and a wash-bowl filled with cold water on top of a small console.

Each morning the bell woke us up at 6 am. Our day begun by cleaning our room before ourselves. The doors would be unlocked for us to stand in line in order to empty our wash-bowl and chamber pot.

We had to control our bowel movement during the night, there was no permission to use the chamber pot, otherwise we would have to expect punishment.

Each morning at 7 am the daily hour of bible study and Prayers was held by Mother Superior in a small chapel, together with all 150 inmates from 5 different groups.

Some of us became asked to get up in front of the group to state certain quotations from the bible by heart we had to learn the night before.

We always were afraid that one self could be chosen and fail.

Failure always meant punishment, and the hardest one was known as "Karzer" or "Butze", a tiny lock up located in the attic.

There was no mattress, nothing to do but sit on a chair and read the bible, sometimes over days or even weeks. Not to be able to communicate is one thing, but being isolated from the group with nothing to do, not to be able to lay down, is the most cruel punishment one can imagine.

This kind of punishment usually being used after one had tried to run away.

Our daily attire was a combination of a long grey dress, an apron and slippers made from felt. We had to knit our 8 monthly sanitary napkins out of heavy cotton yarn, marked with our personal number.

They became washed each month after use and returned to each individual girl. I had to use mine for my entire stay at the reformatory.

There was no educational teaching at the institution, no medical examinations, only lectures of the bible.

Only once, at the beginning of my incarceration I had an examination to find out if I still was a virgin. The entire complex was fenced by a huge wall. When ever we had left the building, we had to wear wooden shoes.

During summertime we were ordered to collect potato beetles and later the potatoes off a farmer's fields.

Sometimes I was selected to a small group to pick blue berries. Afterwards we had to show our tong to prove we had not consumed any berries.

As little girl I was brought up according to Nazi doctrine. The same education continued at the Reformatory.

I have experienced and lived my own concentration camp.

Heike Freiwald

EHEMALIGE

HEIMKINDER

My Poems

Cordially by Heike Freiwald

Confession

Forgive me my Father for all those years
when I felt like a wanderer,
ignoring your love while lost in my fears.

So many people have crossed my way,
where was my smile to comfort their day?
Have I been blind, unable to see
the little sparrow up in the tree? –
Reminding the world with his simple song
that you are the power that makes us strong.

Strong for this world, with love for each other
believing in you and your Son, my Father.
You did not forget me, nor turned away,
please, try me once more and help me to stay.

I know I'm not strong, but willing to try,
to please you my Father, and not make you cry.

Cornfields

I strolled through cornfields with the wind
but sunshine in my heart.
I touched the crop real gently
while pushing it apart.

I hope, I did not hurt it
while being just a child.

I only felt it's beauty –
please, make your judgement mild.

Friends?

Meanless words to be wiped away
by the broom of my mind –
I have nothing to say.
The room seems pregnant by its verbal waste
it disturbs my feelings
and questions my taste.

I call them friends whose eyes filled with lies
whose empty bodies are willing to try conversation –
in simple words: a result of frustration that only hurts.
I look around me
to reach for a smile –
and get lost in the dog, that had rest for a while.

Grandfather

You fought as a soldier in the trenches of France
longing for freedom, for laughter , for dance
strong as a tree, almost bursting for pride
the man with the wide-open heart on my mind.

You took my hand and helped me to see:
the flowers, the fish, the birds in the tree
the smile of the sun that created the shadow
the small little snake at the edge of the meadow.

You read me the stories of the father of waters
the Indians, the war, about coalminers daughters
I set on your knees only four years old
imagining the places I have been told.

You opened my heart for the beauty for love,
for people and my heavenly Father above.

But now I am lost, oh love of my life,
please, send me your wisdom and help me to strive
after things I saw with your eyes as a kid –
I need you, my grandfather – as I always did.

I finally belong

I wrote my name into the soil,
I finally belong –
with moving grain in endless fields,
aged trees still standing strong.
Where countless birds will sing their song
while darkening the sky
where beauty means a flower –
all fragile, rather shy.

I wrote my name into the soil,
I finally feel free –
where stormy winds with all their might
have taught me, made me see
and understand the meaning of
freedom in their song.
I wrote my name into the soil
I finally belong.

In memory of Lina
Farm Centennial · September 4, 1994

Inner Freedom

The breath I took, the first in life was given to me free
but place of birth and fatherland determined destiny.
My cradle, carved from German wood, the strongest of all trees,
demanded faith and true beliefs in nationality.

As a little girl I had to learn
the facts that make us strong,
perfection, strength and power
I had to take along.

A certain age then brought a doubt
it questioned my beliefs
an unknown need for freedom
had come for my relief.

I searched for love – but did not know
to reach for, get it free
without to bargain with my strength and capability.

I searched and searched a long, long time
and finally I prayed
that I might gain the wisdom,
to overcome all hate.

A hate I felt inside of me,
resulting from doctrines,
I had obeyed in all those years
with pride and lack of means.

My prayers have been answered
and freedom I do see,
the love I once so yearned for
is now inside of me.

Sometimes I do remember those years, and have to sigh
remembering the strongest rule:
a NAZI CHILD has not to cry.

Grace of Age

I wonder when the age will knock with power on my door
if I shall open gracefully, the way I did before –
Gave entrance to the woman who'd left the youth behind,
like spring had changed to summer, all gentle, soft and kind.

I wonder if I'll open up when winter changes fall,
I know, I will be older then, I've lived the seasons, changed them all.

I wonder if I'll open up with fear upon my face –
will wisdom wipe my tears away ... and light my face with grace?

Journey of my heart

Christmas is the season, but rain is falling down
my heart is on a journey, home to my little town
far, far across the ocean, so many miles from here
I'm thinking of my father I have not seen for years.

Christmas is the season, and Christ is born again
my heart is on a journey, home to this poor old man
who's waiting like the others, by sharing all their pain
in longing for their children for coming home again.

Christmas is the season, and I'm alone like you
my heart is on a journey, it's coming home to you.
I'm in a foreign country, so many miles away, I'm longing for you, father
but know, I have to stay.

Forever Burden

The burden never left me, no matter how I tried
to free my soul, my conscience from nightmares on my mind.
From pictures of atrocity, committed by a man
I knew as "Uncle Adolf" – I had to say his name
to please and tease (in innocence) his most loyal fan for years,
the man who was my Father, the one I loved through tears.

Insanity

... a breath away from you, or maybe me
an artist with the need to paint, but unable to see.

Insanity –
an awkward term for people off the ground
the poor old fool up on the hill who listens to the sound.

Insanity –
a step away from those who try to see the beauty in a little bird that just
had left its tree.

Insanity –
a gentle touch for those who came to earth
with deepest darkness in their mind, unqualified from birth.

Insanity –
has reached my life a moment close from soon
a friendly hand I've waited for
to help me face the ruin.

Lady of Sensation

Berlin – Berlin, you beautiful old Lady of sensation, once glorified
                                                    throughout the land,
First Lady of the nation.
Those endless years of senseless war have kept some wrinkles on your
                                                                face –
your punishment by alien law was ment for us, who had lost their face.

You took the burden, our blame, to free us from the shame –
the chance for us, a brand new start, to feel reborn again.

Berlin – Berlin you beautiful old Lady of sensation, still glorified
                                    throughout the land as mother of the nation.
With tears of hope and strong beliefs for peace you proudly stand
enduring our punishment, barbed wire at your hand.

There still moves war around the world, your wall dividing friends
I wish they all could visit you to learn and understand the dignity and
                                                    grace you've kept,
old Lady of sensation –
by reaching out your hurting hand in friendship to all nations.

(1983)

Loneliness

I was wandering the street of life
and recognized the loneliness in the shadow of my steps.
Then sunshine broke the soaring clouds
to embrace my hungry spirit.
Butterflies tumbled around me
and strengthened my weak body.
Pretty flowers opened their blossoms
and welcomed my salty tears
to melt them with their sweet aroma.

Power of mind

My body seems tired from exhausting years
from being a woman who's lost in her fears.
From fighting for freedom of body and mind
the need for attention and someone to find.
My body seems tired and ready to rest
the shell of a woman who had given her best.

But there is my mind
that shows the direction, still eager to fight
and in search of attraction.
I might be tired, almost ready to die –
the power of mind keeps me up, standing high.

Simplicity

Simplicity would change this world
could people only see
the meaning of some little things that keep our spirit free.
To smell a flower, modest white, a leaf moved by the rain
the poor old man who'd crossed the street
his face is marked by pain.

If we would treasure beauty, free given by each day
we would not need to fight for things
we had a chance to stay
together and survive this world of hunger caused by greed
for things who have no meaning:
like ink without a sheet.

The Child

The mother lies buried in flowers all wild
to say goodbye to the daily light.
She lies there so peaceful, so quiet and still
she cannot feel that she never will see once more her little child
which had entered the room from playing all wild
to tell Mom: I love you and asked with a smile ...
please, give me one flower, and let us play for a while.
When mother keeps quiet, all peaceful and still,
the child thinks she sleeps, but surely she will ...
It closes the door, real softly it seems
for not disturbing its mother's dreams.

Sunset

The moment when the sun has kissed the surface, far off shore –
when purple reds have changed the day
and make me linger for
some happy fish who jump for joy to fetch the sinking light,
creating moving circles, their welcome to the night.
The moment when the shadow moves away from me, to dark,
when all the birds have sung their song
and left behind a spark inside my ear and inner soul
I realize once more ...
another day will vanish soon, give entrance to the moon.

Little Stranger

Little stranger at the fence, don't look at me that way –
I love the sun, the flowers too
I'm begging you to stay
and share with me my German toy
and if you smile, I'll sing
in simple words a foreign song
of butterflies in spring.

Sheer Beauty

A moment of sheer beauty has touched me once before
it left behind some teardrops, a bitter taste of freedom
at walks on empty shores.
This moment of confusion has changed my wants for more
to linger in illusion in front of silent doors.

Epilogue

Post-war Germany did not change the former teachings of Nazi Germany Institutional children who had been released from Reformatories and experienced the cruel attitude how society related to their past.

We were called "Freiwild" – our new status by the German male population who tried to take advantage of our reputation as bad or fallen girls. In their imagination we were easy to target, willing to have sex. There is no translation to "Freiwild" related to people, only to animals, meaning "open hunt season".

I was 19 years of age at my release from the Reformatory, on my way to work for a farmer and his family residing in a tiny village close to my home. To leave the fenced-in premise behind did not unleash the euphoric outburst I had dreamed of. To be released from the Reformatory did not mean to be free. One had to be 21 years old to be of age by German law; therefore I still was under social supervision.

Well, I was free in a way that I was able to talk without permission, free to wear my own cloth and shoes, free to keep some small possessions, free to inhale fresh air, and free in search of beauty.

The family on the farm operated the only small convenient store in the village. The business, connected with a bakery was situated in front of the building. I was given different daily chores accumulating long hours of hard work. My pay was sent to the Reformatory, leaving me with small pocket money.

I had to share my room with an older female laborer who was kind to me and helped to make the time some easier. In the early evening the front door became locked, and sometimes the maid and I escaped through the chicken cube in order to take a swim at the close pond.

Well, I guess it had to happen after several weeks of hard work at the farm. The farmer's attitude towards me had changed, his behavior sent unspoken sexual desire, and his talk involved suggestive remarks.

When I informed my social worker about the situation, she admonished me to act more restrained.

No matter how I reserved I became, the more the farmer went after me. One day he pushed me into a corner and I yelled for help. I had sensed his wife's anger and jealousy towards me for a while because her husband's attitude had become too obvious. I guess she couldn't bare it any longer, called me words unsuited for a woman. I was told again that I was nothing, but a bad and worthless person, unfit for society –, another reason to become locked up again?

This time I found myself behind bars in a real prison with two other women in one cell. In order to get rid of me, the farmer's wife had accused me for having embezzled money. It was her word against mine, and there was nothing I could say or do. Somehow I was glad to be away from that couple, and somehow I thought by myself it couldn't get much worse.

I sent letters to my father which never became answered. Nobody believed a girl with a past who was released several months earlier from a Reformatory. Well, not that I had given up, it just felt that nothing mattered anymore. I had survived three years in a Reformatory, and I would survive two more years in prison if I had to, until I would become of age.

Shortly before Christmas I was told I had a visitor, but no clue about anyone who had come for a visit. To my parents I had died long time ago, and my sister never had answered any of my letters either. I always had talked to my beloved grandfather after he had passed when I was young. His unconditional love had guided me through my darkest hours, and I still believe he would watch after me from above.

At first I was unable to place the person who sat across the table inside the visitation room. It was a former neighbor who had always trusted me to baby-sit his children before I spent time at the Reformatory. He had met my father and found out about my imprisonment and decided to come for a visit after my father had told him that he did not have a daughter any more.

That very day I realized that for the first time after many years an almost stranger had come to see me, to talk and to be kind to me.

A few weeks later the prison doors opened for my release. I never had a trial, and I never had a police record either. The farmer's wife had admitted to have made a mistake. During those years no one believed a former institutional girl to be innocent if accused by an adult of wrong-doing. One was alone to battle anger, disappointment, unfairness or even hate.

My former neighbor and his wife gave me a new home, and came spring I got married to their nephew, a good looking pilot candidate in the German military. I was completely in love, obedient and tried to be a good mother after my first son was born a year later.

Within my marriage I raised two children, took care of my husband and became the perfect "Hausfrau". During my marriage I made a big mistake, I smothered my husband with too much love I had stored while being locked up.

My husband resembled the vision of former Nazi ideology about the perfect German man: blond hair, blue eyes, tall and capable of following orders.

I finally realized that unconsciously I had adapted my father's teachings in my search for beauty. My devotion towards the father of my children had left me feeling empty inside and doubtful about myself.

During my marriage I had tried to improve my knowledge by reading informative books and got interested in the beauty of arts.

I wasn't satisfied by being just a mother, there still was something missing that might make me feel better and improve my self-esteem.

All of my life I had obeyed orders for various reasons. This time I was able to do something about it. I wanted to show the world that I was not a loser, and I was in need for being respected from the people next to me, my children.

A well-known German Art Academy offered scholarships to gifted students who never had the chance for a higher education.

The acceptance to become a student involved two days of testing in all-round education, drawing, sculpting and discussions with art teachers, professors and student body.

I was one of 18 future students to be chosen from 180 applicants.

That very day changed my future life.

I left my husband, took my two sons and became an art student at the Art Academy to study design.

My husband did not allow anything to take besides the children.

His comment: "You didn't own anything when we met, you can't take anything with you."

Before I found a place to live I shared an apartment with some students and jobbed at night in a restaurant in order to buy the necessary things for our own place.

It wasn't an easy start in our new life, but the three of us managed with our simple lifestyle and lack of possessions.

I finally had gained self-esteem and the needed self-confidence to be around people who accepted me and the boys who became integrated in the anti-authoritarian Kindergarten at the Art Academy.

The influential time of the late 60s had changed my life totally.

My acceptance at the academy had taught me to be gifted, meaning, to be special. I remembered the suggestive words my father always told me that I was special because blue blood run through my veins.

Those words belonged to faded memories that had no longer impact on my life.

This was reality, and the experiences of reality would mark my life, but more important, it would mark the personality of the three of us.

The existence of my kids provided the everyday new strength to keep on going.

Throughout the years I was not capable of keeping a relationship. Like I said, I did leave before I got hurt. During my former marriage I had experienced a relationship in which one person was the giver and the other the loser. I was willing to give everything and lost my self-respect.

In my search for beauty I had become a perfectionist, unable to tolerate disorder, the only straw to balance my unsettled life.

My entire life had turned into a roller coaster, one experience after another, always on the move, running against the wind. It was a result of early treatment by German society during my childhood that did not fit my grandfather's teachings, nor my idealistic view of life. I had forwarded Friederich's wisdom on to my children, told them the same stories I was told by him while a kid, preserving his legacy.

A mother is always part of society due to certain rules and laws. There are times I can feel the pressure of guilt for not having played by the rules. Myself I had experienced the toughest, strictest rules of former Nazi doctrine, being screwed by the government, church and society.

My time at the Art Academy did not entirely erase the knowledge about the past of my father that had left a heavy burden on my shoulder. I did not know where to belong, I was restless and in search of a place to settle down.

The father of my children removed himself from his responsibility and never paid any child support.

There was no one I could lean on; I was the only person to take care of my boys. I did miss my grandfather, the only person who gave his love without any expectation for something in return.

His knowledge and teachings about life had brought me this far and certainly would accompany me on my search for inner peace and freedom on my future path.

Looking back into my past I have to admit that my life has been very unusual, almost impossible to understand or to accept for a regular person.

I was restless, always on the move, running away before hurt could get a hold of me. The sole responsibility to my children and three years of psychic stress had left its toll. I was exhausted but more determined than ever to prove that I could handle my responsibility as a mother. Without my children I probably would have ended my life like so many former institutionalized children before me.

During my marriage I had experienced the rules: one is the winner and the other one who gives everything becomes the loser. Does that mean that giving love means weakness in the eyes of the partner?

During my future life I was incapable to keep a relationship. I became tough and lived by my own rules, not willing to let former rules of my early life interfere with the teachings of my grandfather. Friederich's unconditional love and teachings had formed my being and provided the basic to my needs.

I wanted to continue and forward his legacy on to my children, the way an honest but simple went-through life, a man who dedicated his entire being to love, people and The Good Lord. He always had been my role model, and he still provided comfort when I reached for him.

Society, rules and law still have an impact on a mother, the reason I often felt guilty about raising my children. I did not live by the rules. I was running against the wind, trying to distant myself from people who had ruled my youth with cruelty and former Nazi doctrine. I had to dislike society; on the other hand I tried so hard to become acknowledged and accepted throughout my work.

After I had finished my studies I moved to Berlin to take a job as a manager of a famous Art Gallery, worked in restaurants and dobbed movies.

In 1977 I moved with my children to Ibiza, Spain, our very first vacation and distance from Germany. I designed and created one of a kind women's fashion to be sold at the Hippie Market.

A year later I left Europe with my children for the United States and moved to Tennessee, sponsored by a former Senator of Tennessee.

I enrolled in Introduction to Building Construction at State Tech. and provided an income by designing and sewing one of a kind women's fashion besides my study.

1980 I opened my own fashion boutique, sponsored by a husband of my best customer. Due to my income I was able to provide for my children and I brought them up accordingly in memory to my grand-father.

The United States became the country I wanted to live. It was the fulfillment of an early childhood dream when grandpa read the stories about the Mississippi, about buffaloes roaming on the prairie and native Indians living off the land, the land of milk and honey.

This unknown society turned out to be friendly, kind and generous, interested in my well-being about myself and my children.

In 1987 I remarried and moved with my husband to California where I was involved with several fashion boutiques, selling my own designs.

Due to my husband's job we moved to various states.

From Corona Del Mar, CA. to Omaha NE., to be close to his company he worked for. I helped my husband to advance into upper management and accompanied him around the world to set up subsidiaries for his company.

We decided to buy the centennial farm from his father who had bought it from his father. The farm was settled in the middle of the prairie in South Dakota, close to an Indian reservation, with lots of land and several barns, surrounded by old trees and the beauty of nature. The barns were built to store hey and corn, the feed for the animals. Some sheds had been used to store grain, farm implement and tools. The farm house itself was built from wood and still resembled the bygone era of the 20th.

To me this was the place I had longed for, the place I belong.

I had fallen in love again with the simplicity of beauty, the land and the animals.

This was my home, and I decided it had to be changed into its own purpose and interior, to resemble simplicity, to look like the original working farm of the 20th.

We still lived in Omaha NE., and whenever there was time between traveling I drove to the farm to fulfill my vision. It took me almost an entire decade to finish my dream, to change the centennial farm back to the area of the 20th combined with its interior design and surroundings.

A few years later we retired to the farm and entertained many friends and former business partners. It was the most beautiful time of my life, involving hard work and freely given beauty by nature. My dream finally came true.

When I walked around the premise and looked inside the barns I visualized the same tools and equipment I memorized seeing at my grandfather's place.

During the change of the century I had removed myself from the public and relatives of my husband. I got sick with depression and panic attacks, leading to a separated daily life between the two of us.

I left and started a new century on my own, homesick for the beauty of the land, the freedom and happiness I once lived.

*This autobiography is dedicated
to my children, Nils and Patrick.*

Heike Freiwald

Unentlohnte Zwangsarbeiter: Bundesrepublik Deutschland, 1960er Jahre.

Bügelsaal im Dortmunder Vincenzheim des katholischen Orden der Barmherzigen Schwestern vom Heiligen Vincent von Paul (ähnlich den "Magdalene Sisters" in Irland und anderen Ländern der Welt mit ihren Großwäschereien wo Mädchen ebenso versklavt wurden).
Unentlohnte Zwangsarbeit in der BRD: Mehr Fotos zwangsarbeitender Jungen und Mädchen im damaligen Westdeutschland können im Internet gefunden werden bei einer BILDER-Suche in GOOGLE nach heimkinder-ueberlebende.

(Bildquelle: Archiv/Heike Freiwald)

Gedenkstein von Peter Dinkel (ehemaliges Heimkind)

(Bildquelle: Archiv/Heike Freiwald)

www.tredition.de

Über tredition

EIN EIGENES BUCH VERÖFFENTLICHEN
tredition wurde 2006 in Hamburg gegründet. Seitdem hat tredition mehrere tausend Buchtitel veröffentlicht. Autoren veröffentlichen in wenigen leichten Schritten gedruckte Bücher, e-Books und audio-Books. tredition hat das Ziel, die beste und fairste Veröffentlichungsmöglichkeit für Autoren zu bieten.

tredition wurde mit der Erkenntnis gegründet, dass nur etwa jedes 200. bei Verlagen eingereichte Manuskript veröffentlicht wird. Dabei hat jedes Buch seinen Markt, also seine Leser. tredition sorgt dafür, dass für jedes Buch die Leserschaft auch erreicht wird.

Im einzigartigen Literatur-Netzwerk von tredition bieten zahlreiche Literatur-Partner (das sind Lektoren, Übersetzer, Hörbuchsprecher und Illustratoren) ihre Dienstleistung an, um Manuskripte zu verbessern oder die Vielfalt zu erhöhen. Autoren vereinbaren direkt mit den Literatur-Partnern die Konditionen ihrer Zusammenarbeit und partizipieren gemeinsam am Erfolg des Buches.

Das gesamte Verlagsprogramm von tredition ist bei allen stationären Buchhandlungen und Online-Buchhändlern wie z. B. Amazon erhältlich. e-Books stehen bei den führenden Online-Portalen (z. B. iBookstore von Apple oder Kindle von Amazon) zum Verkauf.

Jetzt ein Buch veröffentlichen: **www.tredition.de**

EINE BUCHREIHE ODER VERLAG GRÜNDEN

Seit 2009 bietet tredition sein Verlagskonzept auch als sogenanntes "White-Label" an. Das bedeutet, dass andere Personen oder Institutionen risikofrei und unkompliziert selbst zum Herausgeber von Büchern und Buchreihen unter eigener Marke werden können. tredition übernimmt dabei das komplette Herstellungs- und Distributionsrisiko.

Zahlreiche Zeitschriften-, Zeitungs- und Buchverlage, Universitäten, Forschungseinrichtungen, u.v.m. nutzen diese Dienstleistung von tredition, um unter eigener Marke ohne Risiko Bücher zu verlegen.

Alle Informationen im Internet: **www.tredition.de/Buchverlage**

tredition wurde mit mehreren Innovationspreisen ausgezeichnet, u. a. Webfuture Award und Innovationspreis der Buch-Digitale.
tredition ist Mitglied im Börsenverein des Deutschen Buchhandels.

Zeitfracht Medien GmbH
Ferdinand-Jühlke-Straße 7
99095 Erfurt, Deutschland
produktsicherheit@kolibri360.de